MISBEHAVE

SHOTGUN FALLS SHIFTERS

AVA BENTON

LIBBY BERNARD

1

———

"Really, Olivia, I don't think it's too much to ask for you to come home for your father's funeral."

Olivia squeezed her eyes shut as tight she could manage while pinching the bridge of her nose between her thumb and forefinger. It was way too early in the day for a headache. "I'm tired of going around in circles about this."

"He was your father."

"No kidding. So *that's* why the two of us looked so much alike."

Her mother's gasp left Olivia wincing harder than ever—and reminding herself why certain thoughts were better left unexpressed, especially when her drama queen of a mother was involved. "That is disgusting. How can you be so blasé?"

"It's taken a lot of practice." That wasn't a joke, either. It had taken years of disciplining herself, training herself out of caring what the man did, thought, or said. Years of ignoring mention of him in the news, to say nothing of the number of times she'd dug her nails into her palms while her mother droned on and on over the latest gossip about him.

She looked at her palms then, seated in her office while her mother berated her over the phone. The absence of crescent-shaped scars was almost surprising.

"I might even be a little bit ashamed of you right now."

That stung. Olivia gritted her teeth against the rising wave of resentment born from guilt. No matter how old she got, no matter how hard she worked on herself, there was never any avoiding guilt from her mother. "He didn't treat me any better than he treated you after the divorce. I know you like to pretend that didn't happen, but I don't have your talent for pretending. Or forgetting."

"That's water under the bridge."

"For you, maybe. And I'm glad for you, I am. But we are not the same."

"That much is clear."

She took a deep breath and, not for the first time, decided to be the bigger person. They weren't going to get anywhere with all this arguing, and unlike her mother, she had a busy day ahead of her at work. It would be better to smooth things over for now. "Mom, I'm sorry I'm not there to support you, I really am. I know this is a difficult day. But as much as I want to be there for you, I can't bring myself to show up at the man's funeral and pretend to feel things I no longer do. Call it self-preservation, but I disconnected myself from him a long time ago." Years after he had done the disconnecting in the first place, but she left that part out for the sake of ending the argument.

"But he's being buried today."

"I have to keep my promise."

"Your promise. I swear you inherited a lot more from that man than your looks. You're just as stubborn and vindictive as him."

"Gee, I can't imagine why I wouldn't want to go to his funeral, then. Because you're right, he was vindictive."

"What's the point of keeping a promise to someone when they're dead? It wasn't exactly a nice promise, either." Her mother snorted disdainfully.

Olivia could picture her wearing her best black dress, pearls, the whole nine yards. Had there been enough time to stop in at the salon to have her roots dyed blonde? "Who promises their father they won't show up for their funeral when the time comes?"

"A girl who watched her mother crumble after he walked out. I watched you crumble again when news of his little girlfriend came out. Then the wedding. Do I have to go on? Because we could talk about the way he dicked you over with the divorce settlement, too."

"Olivia."

"Mom. Are we finished with this? Not to cut you off, but I did apologize, and there's no hope of my getting out there in time for the services at this point, anyway. So this is entirely moot."

"And you don't care how it looks?"

"I couldn't care less. You're the one who always cares about how things look, remember?"

"Sometimes I'd swear you do and say things just to upset me." Olivia rolled her eyes while her mother sniffled. "You know, you can't avoid this forever. Some of your father's lawyers from the company have reached out and said they needed to speak to you."

"If they need to speak to me, they know where to

find me." With that, she cleared her throat. "I've got to go. I have a meeting in a few minutes. Good luck at the funeral." An awkward thing to say, but what did a person say before getting off the phone on a day like this?

As cruel as her mother might think she was, there were much worse things she could have said. She could've asked whether Priscilla Barnes, much-maligned first wide, understood how pathetic it would look for her to break down weeping at the graveside, which of course she would because that was how she had conducted most of her life. Big emotions, grand gestures, whatever kept the spotlight on her. And those seated nearby might offer comfort, old friends who would murmur their apologies and pat her hand while inwardly laughing or rolling their eyes. They had been divorced longer than they'd been married, and the man had another wife. And he had certainly not held his tongue in the years since the divorce. One of the few mercies Olivia granted her mother was the way she didn't repeat cruel gossip about the shrill, grasping woman her father had once been married to.

There was a sharp knock at Olivia's door before her assistant poked her head in. "Five minutes."

"Thank you, Lauren."

Their usual five-minute warning. Enough time to get her head in the game and away from memories and bitterness that thoughts of her father always stirred up. Thinking about him wasn't going to get her anywhere when she had a presentation to make. Of all days for Mom to call and give her hell. The idea was to run over the presentation and make sure she was comfortable with the delivery before going in and running over her team's numbers in front of the company's CEO. It was a lot of pressure, being the company's youngest editor and a woman to boot, but pressure was one thing she'd always thrived on.

No matter how pleased she was with their performance over the past year, at the end of the day all that mattered was making sure the higher-ups knew about it. No time for false modesty, no under-selling. If there was one lesson she'd picked up from her father, it was that. *In business, there's no room for undervaluing yourself.* Especially as a young woman in what was still very much a man's world.

She hopped up and dashed to the ladies' room for a quick touch-up on her hair and makeup. Her straight, black locks were pulled back in a sleek ponytail, and her blue eyes sparkled with excitement. Only in the very back of her mind did she wonder if it was technically right, being this excited about anything on the day of her father's funeral.

She recalled another lesson he'd taught her, whether or not the lesson had been a conscious one: when it came to business, nothing mattered more than getting ahead. Even if it meant pushing family concerns aside.

That lesson he'd drummed into her head from a very early age.

THERE WAS nothing like getting home after a long, successful day. Olivia flipped on the lights before closing the door to the apartment. It was small, but it was hers. She had chosen every piece of furniture, every picture on the wall with painstaking care. She had haunted estate sales, scoured online listings, and piece by piece had put together a cozy, plant-filled home that made her smile every time she stepped foot in the door. At the end of the day, that was all she wanted.

She kicked off her shoes before going to the kitchen and setting down a bag of groceries. After putting away the perishables, she uncorked a bottle of Chablis and poured a generous glass. Buying the bottle was an act of celebration. The presentation had gone like gangbusters, to use the boss's favorite old-timey saying, and she'd gone out after work to pick up a few things for a special dinner. Now there was sushi waiting to be savored and a slice of her favorite cheesecake for later.

But first, a glass of wine to help her unwind— and to dull the lingering sense of spaciness which had plagued her at random times during the day. Whenever she'd had a quiet moment, she'd wonder what her mother was doing. How many people had shown up for the funeral? Would there be anyone she'd remember from her childhood?

One thing she didn't feel was regret. Even that made her think more than she wanted to. Was there something wrong with her that she was able to feel nothing for the man who'd given her life? Then again, she reasoned on her way to the bedroom, what did that mean? So he was her father. He'd removed himself from her life after the divorce. He may as well have forgotten she existed. That wasn't a father. That was a sperm donor.

She laughed at the thought while slipping out of her dress. That was how she needed to think about the late Marcus Pemberton, tech genius and multi-millionaire. The sperm donor whom she'd lived with during childhood. Who'd taken her to Disney-land and ridden the Matterhorn four times in a row because she'd begged him to. Who'd once dressed up like a prince on Halloween because she was a princess, and he was walking her from door to door. Who had always encouraged her love of reading and writing, filling her bedroom with books.

She plopped down on the foot of her bed, still holding her wineglass. When had this turned into a reminiscing session? It was better to forget those times. They clearly had meant nothing to him. How could they have, if he was able to cut himself off and walk away without a backward glance?

A single tear spilled over her lashes, but she was quick to brush it away. No tears. She had already cried enough over the years, back when she was too young to understand. This was supposed to be a night for celebrating, even if she was doing it alone. That was the problem with being the last of her close friends to find a man.

Not that she held it against any of them. The girls deserved everything. All the happiness in the world. She'd always felt like the mother hen of the group, encouraging them to go for the things they wanted out of life. They'd found those things. Char-lotte was still happily managing the dating app she'd helped her fiancé develop. Hope had moved in with her boyfriend and lived near Charlotte now. Megan spent more time out in the wilderness than at home anymore, working with wolves alongside her boyfriend. And now Audra was helping to run an inn with the man who'd recently proposed.

It had been a month since that night, when all the girls and their guys had gotten together to celebrate the inn's reopening—and later, the engagement. Pine Cove was a cute little town, if remote, and Audra had practically glowed with happiness and pride during the tour she'd given them.

Thinking back on it, Olivia had to wonder if that was the last time they'd all be together. Times had changed. The logistics of a girls' weekend to Shotgun Falls made her head spin. It wasn't as simple as getting on group chat and working out a date, especially when Megan was out in the middle of nowhere half the time and Audra was busy cleaning rooms and... whatever else it took to run a bed and breakfast. It would make sense for the girls to gather there and throw a little extra business Audra's way, but it wouldn't exactly be relaxing for her, either. That didn't seem fair.

Good thing she was happy with her life. The presentation had gone well, and all signs pointed to a promotion in her future. With that in mind, and too much sushi and cheesecake in her stomach, she went to bed later that evening feeling happier than she had in a while.

The feeling carried through to the morning. She woke with a smile, got in a ride on her stationary bike while reading through some of the edits one of her clients had made to a book she'd acquired. It was getting there, that book, slowing being smoothed and polished until it shone. She looked forward to continuing her reading once she got to the office. What a gift, looking forward to getting into the office. How many people dreaded it?

She was still reflecting on this as she opened the front door.

Only to be met by three strangers. One of them, the only woman in the group, had been about to knock on the door when Olivia opened it. All three were dressed in dark suits. When the taller of the men raised his hand in greeting, a flashy watch gleamed in the hallway fluorescents.

"Olivia Barnes?"

"Yes." She looked at the three of them in turn. "Who are you?"

The tall man spoke first. "We're with the law firm of Cooper and Schultz, based out of Los Angeles. We served as part of your father's legal team and are here to discuss your father's will."

She folded her arms, eyes narrowing. Would it be better to laugh first or skip straight to the part where she told them to get lost? "I told my mother you'd know where to find me, but I didn't expect you to show up at my front door the morning after the funeral."

"Miss Barnes, I'm Vanessa Merkle." Was she brought along to soften things up? To provide a sprinkling of female understanding? "In a situation such as this, we find it necessary to expedite the process."

"And why is that? I don't want anything from the man and, frankly, you're about to make me late for work. I need to go. If you want to set up an appointment, I'd be glad to work out a time that will suit all of us."

"Miss Barnes, I don't think you understand." Vanessa slid a look at her colleagues. "You're the sole inheritor of your father's many holdings. Including his company."

2

It was enough to make her fall back a step. "The sole inheritor?"

The tall man jumped in again. "Miss Barnes, my name is Jacob Hawthorne. My colleague is correct. The terms of your father's will are clear. You and you alone have inherited his entire estate, along with ownership of Pemberton Technologies." He withdrew a thick manilla envelope from his briefcase. "We have quite a bit to go through, and then we will require your signature."

"It might be best if we stepped inside." Vanessa looked up at Jacob, wearing the sort of expression a woman wore when a man was screwing everything up.

Meanwhile, Olivia stood in the doorway with her mouth hanging open. Her? He had left everything to her? "I haven't spoken to him in years."

"You'll see once you allow us to go through the paperwork that this is all as we've said." Vanessa wore a tight smile. "The sooner we get this settled, the better for everyone."

"Who is everyone?"

"The company's board of directors, to start with. You may not know this, but PemTech made the Fortune 500 the past three years in a row."

"I was not aware of that." Not that she cared.

"The board holds a responsibility to its investors. Meaning management. Leadership."

"And how is that my problem, just because he decided it should be?" The three of them started speaking at once, which was the last thing she felt like listening to. She held up both hands, shaking her head. "I'm sorry, but I wasn't kidding when I said I need to get out of here. I want nothing to do with my father's company, and I never have."

"He also owns a great deal of land in California, Nevada, and Arizona. Several shipping companies. There's the beachfront property in Malibu, the house in the Keys." It was clear from Jacob's expression he expected her to be impressed. "All of which is now yours."

"What about Melanie? Why didn't he leave all of this to his new wife?" No, the word new didn't quite fit. They'd been married fifteen years. Had it really been that long? Amazing, the idea of him not getting bored with her. Maybe gravity had chosen to ignore her. Either that, or the girl had spent the last decade and a half staying firm, toned, and youthful.

Not youthful enough to inherit his wealth, though.

"We're not at liberty to say." The three of them exchanged looks that didn't inspire confidence. What they did inspire was suspicion. They were holding something back, but what could it be? And why did it concern her?

"That's fine. I don't even need to know. The song remains the same, either way. I don't want anything to do with this. I don't accept it. Don't I get a say?"

The third man who hadn't bothered introducing himself sounded like he was choking. "You would refuse this? Do you realize how much your father was worth at the time of his passing?"

"I don't have the first idea, but I have no doubt you'll want to tell me about it. Like I said, I don't care."

She checked her phone before scowling at all three of them. "I have to go. I'm going to have to ask you to leave, and if you don't leave on your own, I will call building security and have you escorted from the premises."

"At least take these, along with my card. Please call at the first opportunity." Jacob handed her the envelope, then a card which she shoved in her pocket without looking at it. The envelope was what grabbed her attention. It's suddenly looked thicker than before, but that could easily have been the psychic weight of what Olivia now knew was inside. She snatched the envelope from him before closing the door, then locking it as an afterthought. While she doubted they would go so far as to break the door down, it was a silent punctuation mark on a conversation she'd never wanted to have. They muttered to each other before their voices faded to silence.

She looked down at the envelope before tossing it to the coffee table. Why would he do it? Why not his wife or even her mother? And was she completely out of her mind, refusing a fortune like the one she knew her father had possessed? They didn't have to be close friends or even warm acquaintances for her to know the sort of power Marcus had held in Silicon Valley.

He would have to wait until later. She had a life to get back to, a life which her father had cut himself out of. What, did he think she was some poor wretch in need of a handout? Or did he just assume, the way he'd always assumed everything, that she would drop everything now that he'd thrown her a couple of crumbs after years of starvation?

She was still mulling it over, brooding and seething, by the time she reached the office. Putting on a happy face occurred to her as she stepped onto the elevator in the lobby, and she tried to do it when the doors slid shut and left her alone. They were video cameras mounted in two corners of the car, but they'd probably picked up much worse than a girl practicing happy expressions in the reflective metal doors. At least, that was what she told herself.

"Good morning." She waved to the receptionist, who had been bent over what seemed like a secretive sort of phone call before sitting bolt upright when she caught sight of Olivia stepping off the elevator. Her face went a little pale, too. "Are you feeling okay?"

"Oh, yeah. Sure. Just fine." Chloe forced a brittle smile. Olivia turned in the direction of her office. The moment her back was to the reception desk, she heard Chloe murmuring something into her headset. She told herself she was being paranoid, but there weren't many excuses for that sort of awkward interaction that didn't involve being the topic of the conversation. Why, though? She'd gone out for lunch with Chloe several times, but it had been months since the last time they had a serious chat. What was there to gossip about?

Chloe wasn't the only person acting strangely. A group of guys gathered around one of the cubicles on the main floor stopped talking when she walked past. A couple of them followed her progress down the hall, not bothering to hide their curiosity. There was another conversation taking place in the break room which went silent when Olivia entered the room to slide her leftover sushi into the shared fridge. "How's it going today?" The best she got were a few vague mumbles. It was enough to make her check out her reflection in the microwave as she passed. Nothing hanging out of her nose, no errant pimples that had suddenly reared up in the fifteen minutes it took to drive from her apartment to work.

It took another minute to reach her office and hang up her jacket. No sooner had she finished than in burst Lauren, wide-eyed and flushed. "Why didn't you say anything?" She closed the door, looking stricken.

"Anything about what? What the hell is going on around here today? It's like everybody knows something I don't."

"Your father died. Why didn't you say anything? That's a huge deal. Do you need anything?"

Olivia reached blindly for her chair before settling into it. Good thing, because her knees had suddenly begun to shake. "My father? What are you talking about?"

"Your dad, Marcus Pemberton. That big tech guy out of Silicon Valley. His death is all over the place. You never said anything to any of us. How come?"

Olivia held up one hand, closing her eyes. *Focus. Breathe.* Lauren fell silent, anyway, which was a good thing. There was no way to think with her helpful, if somewhat chatty, assistant going on and on.

One question bubbled up to the surface of her troubled thoughts. "How did you know he was my father? There's a reason I don't use his last name." Instead, she'd chosen to adopt her mother's maiden name, even if Mom hadn't changed it back after the divorce.

She opened her eyes to find Lauren looking worse than before. Olivia considered offering her a seat since she looked like she was ready to drop.

"Tell me you haven't checked any of the news stations today."

"I was reviewing edits this morning." It seemed best to leave out the visit with the lawyers.

Lauren gasped, covering her mouth with one hand. "Oh, damn it. I should have asked you that first. It's just all been such a surprise."

"Can you please tell me what you're talking about? What's been on the news?"

"Pull up CNN." Lauren nodded, indicating Olivia's MacBook which was still closed on her desk. She lifted the lid more out of curiosity at this point and pulled up her browser.

The headline was huge and blunt. *Silicon Valley Tech Guru Cause Of Death Revealed.*

Beneath it were three photos. One was of the man himself, smiling and confident in a suit that probably cost more than some people spent on cars. The second, a photo of herself, the caption naming her Marcus Pemberton's daughter and the heiress to his fortune.

The third photo was the one that stopped the world spinning and brought everything to a standstill. A burnt, blackened wreck of what had at one time been a luxury automobile but was now nothing more than a husk, parts of it lying strewn around the main body.

"Apparently, they were trying to keep the accident under wraps, but somebody leaked it to the press." Somewhere in all of this, Lauren had joined Olivia behind the computer. She placed a hand on her shoulder. "His car exploded when he turned it on in front of his house."

Olivia let out a sound between a gasp and a groan, falling back against the chair. "Nobody told me. I had no idea that was how…"

"Like I said, the article says everybody was hush-hush about how he died." Yes, and Olivia hadn't thought to ask. He was dead, that was all that mattered. Or so she'd told herself when she got the first call from California.

But this? This was something entirely different. Cars didn't randomly explode.

And now, the entire world knew she was his daughter, something she'd worked hard to hide.

As if reading her thoughts, Lauren perched on the corner of the desk wearing a concerned look. "Why didn't you ever tell anybody? Shoot, if my dad was some kind of millionaire genius, I would want everybody to know."

"It's complicated." Of all her problems, that was

the least of them. It was also the last thing she felt like explaining to anyone, even someone as sweet as Lauren. "I think I need a minute to absorb this."

"Of course." Lauren hopped up. "Can I get you anything? Some water, maybe a cup of tea?"

"No, thank you. I'll be fine." She was barely able to wait until the door was closed before jumping up and shoving a hand in her jacket pocket. Jacob's business card was still inside. She punched the numbers into her cell, her hands shaking.

"Miss Barnes. I didn't expect—"

"Why didn't you tell me the full story? Damn it, you were right there at my apartment. You could have told me how he died. Don't pretend you didn't know, either."

He hesitated, the silence stretching out for what felt like hours but couldn't have lasted more than a second or two. "Miss Barnes, with all due respect, we thought you knew. We assumed the media would have reached out to you before word got around."

"Well, surprise, they didn't. Nobody told me. Not even my mother, for God's sake." Though it wasn't outside the realm of possibility that she was just as clueless. "Hell, you didn't even offer me condolences when you showed up out of the blue. What is going on? Why would anybody want to blow up my father's car?"

"I understand your concerns."

"Concerns? Are you joking? This goes a lot deeper than that, buddy." To hell with politeness. Politeness had never gotten her anywhere, anyway. "How long were you my father's legal representatives?"

"For the past ten years or more. I wasn't employed with the firm at the time, but—"

"That's fine. Ten years. I need you to tell me what he got himself into in the past ten years that would leave somebody wanting to blow him sky-high." The article was still pulled up on her computer. She glanced at the screen, and her stomach churned at the sight of the wreckage. It was amazing there was a body left to bury after something like that.

Another pause, longer this time. Anger alone was what kept her on her feet, kept her head clear. Otherwise, she might be on the floor, or with her head in her wastebasket. Explosion. Did he die right away? Was there a moment of awareness before the explosion when he knew it was the end? She shook her head, trying to clear these thoughts. They weren't going to help her.

"Miss Barnes, if you're concerned for your safety,

we are in a position to employ bodyguards for your safety. Your father did make a stipulation for that in his papers, which you'll see when you take the time to review them."

"A bodyguard? Are you kidding me?" She ended the call before slapping the phone down on her desk. That was their solution? Rather than give her the answers she deserved, they wanted to hire a bodyguard and pat her on the head.

And she was supposed to step into her father's shoes? Maybe that was the whole idea. Get to her, get the papers signed, then let her find out her father had enemies willing to blow him up. Which meant they might want to blow her up.

All the more reason to refuse her inheritance. There had to be a way to do that. She closed the tab with the article in favor of Googling. She found that it was, in fact, possible to turn down an inheritance. She would have to sign everything over, but that was what lawyers were for. They could work that out. So long as she stayed out of the company and her father's holdings, she would be okay. She had to believe that.

And as the days went on, that seemed to be true. Except for what felt like hourly phone calls from Jacob, life went on how it normally did. Now that the entire company knew about her connection to Marcus, they seemed ready to tiptoe whenever she came into view. She shut that down whenever it came up. "Don't worry. I'm not going to break." She always said it with as much confidence as she could, and it seemed to be enough to settle everybody's minds. The quicker she got past this, the better.

By Friday, things had gotten pretty much back to normal except for the phone calls she kept ignoring. It might have been easier to block the number, but there was some perverse part of her that wanted to keep track of the number of times the lawyers tried to get a hold of her before they finally got the hint. He never left voicemails, either. She was waiting for the one where he finally broke down and said okay, it's clear you want nothing to do with this, let's find a way to get you out of it. So far, she was disappointed.

"See you on Monday." She waved to a couple of the girls before heading to her car in the lot outside the building. There was nothing like the feeling of getting out on a Friday, even if late meetings had kept her around longer than she wanted to be. After the past week, she wanted nothing more than a long bubble bath and a solid Netflix binge. Preferably while eating some serious junk food. It seemed the least of what she deserved.

That was the thought on her mind as she reached for her keys on coming to the end of the row in which she'd parked. She touched her finger to the fob to unlock her door.

And set off an explosion strong enough to knock her flat on the concrete.

3

"I'm not sure what Drake made it sound like." Xavier took in the cabin, or rather what he could make out from his spot barely inside the front door. He clutched his bag in one hand, uncertain of whether he should set it down or throw it back inside his truck and hit the road again. Why had he allowed Drake to talk him into this?

Nico had let him inside and now waved him further in. "You look like you're ready to run, buddy. You don't trust me?"

"No, no. It's not that."

"What is it? You sense something's off?"

"Everything is off right now, which you well know." Hence his reason for being there.

"Listen. No pressure." Nico dropped the playful,

joking attitude. "Nobody is forcing you to be here. I was only hoping to catch up a little, see how you're doing. Don't hold it against Drake for calling."

"I'll hold it against myself, instead." What was he thinking, spilling his guts? That night at the bar in Pine Cove, where they'd been celebrating the inn reopening. Everybody had been happy, hopeful, especially after Drake's proposal.

What had Xavier chosen to do? He'd gotten drunk—no small feat for a shifter—and unburdened himself. Audra had taken her girlfriends up to the inn for a tour and most of the folks from town had already turned in for the night. For some reason, it had seemed like a great idea to pour his heart out to his old friend.

"You have nothing to hold against yourself. Things like this happen sometimes. Inexplicable things."

"No offense, but you're not making me feel any better. And I already know why it happens." Though he did lower his bag to the floor, which was a step in the right direction. "So long as you think it's safe."

"So long as what is safe?" Audra descended from the second floor, still toweling off her hair after a shower. The scent of shampoo and soap was strong enough to nearly choke him. "Hey. It's so good to see you."

Xavier looked to Nico, lifting an eyebrow. Nico nodded. "She knows."

And she still wanted him there? From all appearances, she seemed at ease. He couldn't scent fear on her, either. Nothing but openness and warmth and apple shampoo.

And it made him feel worse than before. "It's just that I hope you understand what it can mean, having me stay with you. Even for a short time. I never know when these... spells or whatever you want to call them will come over me. Sometimes they come up out of nowhere, and all I can do is ride it out until it's over and hope I haven't hurt anyone."

"I understand." Megan draped the towel around her neck, holding the ends. "I also know what a good heart you have. And you said it yourself when you were talking with Drake. You've never attacked anyone. You may have destroyed a few things or animals, but never people."

"So Drake was kind enough to share that, as well. How fortunate for me." *Drake talks too damn much.* What a stunning reminder of why Xavier had kept his secret to himself for years.

Until the spells started getting worse. And more frequent.

"All it means is you have friends who care about you. I can think of much worse things than that." She whistled softly on her way to the kitchen. "Are you hungry?"

"Actually, I thought maybe Xavier and I could step outside to talk for a while." Nico left no room for discussion, practically shoving Xavier out the door while wearing a smile. "Let me know when you get dinner started, and we'll be sure to put this guy to work."

Once they were outside, he dropped the act again. "I could feel you getting up in your emotions in there. I thought maybe we could get a breath of fresh air instead of letting her see it."

"It's that obvious?"

"Only to you and me. Even a human who spends her life studying wolves doesn't know what it's like to be one." They settled in the rocking chairs positioned on either side of a table on which a chess game had been set up. If he cared about things like that, it might've struck him as sort of nice. A reminder of his friend's domestic bliss. "So tell me about it. What's going on? How the hell did you keep a secret this long?"

"To answer your second question, the rages were rarer until a few months ago. That's when they started

ramping up. It's become harder to hide. Almost impossible to concentrate on anything."

He sank back in the chair with a groan. "I've heard people talk about withdrawing from nicotine, and it's the closest way I can think of to describe what I feel all the time. Every waking moment. Like my mind is always, constantly waiting for something. Waiting for that switch to flip in my head." Xavier snapped his fingers, the sound crisp and sharp. "I'm never fully in the moment no matter what I'm doing or where I am. All I can think about is that helpless feeling when I know I'm about to lose control. There's nothing I can do about it but wait until it's over. And try to get me away from people."

"Did you ever go see Micah and his mate?"

"Esme? I saw her a few days ago, up at their cabin. If I ever thought I'd see the day Micah would be mated with a witch..." He chuckled, shaking his head.

"Had we known he was part warlock himself, we might have at least suspected the possibility."

Xavier continued to gaze out at the expanse laid

out before him. The woods were gorgeous, dense and lush, pines towering like they wanted to touch the sky. The sun was beginning to sink, painting the peaks amber and gold. If he could only find somewhere like this to live on his own, he might be able to rest at night. Knowing there would be few chances to hurt another person, be they human or shifter.

He could feel Nico's penetrating gaze and knew he wouldn't get away with changing the subject. "There was nothing she could do."

"Was she sure?"

"She's already proven how talented she is. Remember when Ezra lost his wolf because of that witch's curse?"

"Right. She cast a spell on him."

"It was Esme who pulled him out of that. That's where she excels, up here." He tapped a finger to his temple. "But try as she would, there was nothing she could plant in my brain to stop it."

"You know what caused it."

It wasn't a question. Why would it be? Drake had already shared the story. "The inoculations they gave me before I went overseas. Before that, I was fine. Normal. That night, after they stuck me with all those needles, I got sick. Very sick. The first rage took me the following afternoon."

"Did something change to make it kick up like this? You said it's gotten worse."

"Around six months ago, I was out on the hunt. Alone." He sighed, the picturesque scene before his turning into something from his memory. Dark, moonlit, the air almost unbearably fresh. The sounds of night creatures scampering in the darkness, so clear to his wolf ears. He could hear them for what felt like miles all around, far enough that they couldn't sense his presence.

"I had hunted my fill. The sun was about to rise, so I returned to the truck and shifted back. Then, I don't know why, but not a hundred yards away a fawn came prancing out into the clearing. I saw her, but I was standing downwind. I guess that's why she didn't notice me. And, I don't know..."

"It's alright. You don't have to explain it."

"I want to." It came out too sharp, enough that Nico winced. "Sorry. If I'm ever going to make sense of this, I have to talk about it. Maybe I'll say the right thing to the right person and it will come together."

"I understand."

"I don't know what happened. My blood felt hot. My skin flushed and suddenly I was sweating. My heart." He tapped his closed fist against his chest like a triphammer. "I thought it would burst out of me.

And all I could keep doing was staring at that fawn. I needed to kill that fawn. Not because I was hungry, because I had to kill. I had to destroy. The whole world went red and before I knew it I was the wolf again, and I was chasing down that fawn and then I tore it to pieces."

"Damn."

"I came to covered in blood. Disgusted with myself. I remember doing it, too. Ripping the body to pieces, shredding it with my claws and my teeth. But at the time, it was like watching myself from outside of myself."

"I understand that. It must have been unnerving."

"Something like that." There were a few words that hit closer. Terrifying being one of them. Watching himself create havoc without the power to stop. "Since then, it's happened at random times. Once I was in the middle of watching TV. Another time, I was on my way out the door to grab a few things from the store. I'm glad I took a few extra minutes getting ready, or it might have happened when I was out on the street."

"Has it ever happened in front of humans?"

"Do you think we would be sitting here together if it had? That was part of the reason I felt confident enough to visit Drake when he was having prob-lems. With him living in Pine Cove and it being the off-season for tourists, it felt safer. Shotgun Falls is still too close to the pack's territory to be safe. I could fly into a rage and shift and run down the middle of Wolf Street. Even Pine Cove's commercial area is practically in the middle of the woods, so a stray wolf wouldn't be too terrifying."

"A stray wolf certainly wouldn't be out of the ordinary up here. That's why we live here now in the first place."

"How is your work going?" Anything, so long as they took a break from peering into his wounded psyche.

"Honestly?" Nico couldn't fight back a grin. "It's great. We spend half our time camping and checking in with the packs. Megan uses me as her translator, so to speak. No sign of poachers in the area. Things couldn't be better."

"I'm glad to hear that."

"Now, we just have to get you taken care of. I would hate to see you shut out the rest of the world because you're afraid of what would happen if you lost control at the wrong time."

"I've considered going solo. Getting behind the wheel and going. Better yet, taking it on foot. That way, I don't have to wonder if I'll shift while driving down the Interstate."

Nico's brows drew together as he sat up straighter, his teeth grinding all the while. Xavier knew the announcement would be met this way. "Where would you go?"

"I haven't thought through it. Besides, the idea of a plan like this is not to give it too much thought." He lowered his brow at his old friend. "And to make sure other people don't try to follow you."

"I can't accept that. Allowing a member of the pack to go rogue. You can't disappear."

"It seems to me that if I decide to disappear, that's my business. Would you rather have me carry the weight of knowing I destroyed someone's life in the middle of one of these rages?"

"You know I wouldn't."

"We can agree on that much."

"And there's nothing Esme can do? She's sure of that?"

Pressure built in Xavier's head. His wolf was restless, which always seemed to be the case anymore. Now, it was the thought of Esme's suggestion that had his hackles rising. "There was one possibility she floated, but it would never work."

"What did she say?"

"Since this isn't a magic-based problem, magic can't undo it—but she could cage the wolf." He used air quotes around the word. An ugly, brutal word for someone like him.

"A cage? I don't understand."

"Up here." He tapped his head again. "Locking him away. I wouldn't be able to shift at will, or at all unless she removed the spell. It would eliminate the problem."

"But it also might make things worse. Wolves don't react well to being trapped."

"Which is exactly why I shot the idea down. Micah backed me up on it so she knows it's not personal."

Nico stroked his jaw, staring out at the darkening sky. "I still can't get on board with the idea of you going away. I'm sorry, I don't like it. It's not natural. We're part of the pack."

"Yet here you are, half a day's drive away from the pack."

"That's different."

"How?"

"Because I could still drive half a day—less than that, in fact—and get back there if there's trouble. People know how to reach me, too. That's also helpful. Just because I'm not there physically all the time doesn't mean I've left."

"The pack doesn't need me, the way I am."

"You should stop speaking for others. Why don't you let them make their own decisions?"

He drew a breath, prepare to argue, his temper rising. It was a good thing the door flew inward when it did, and a moment later Megan stumbled onto the porch.

Nico was out of his chair in an instant, followed by Xavier. It didn't take a wolf's senses to see she was in distress. She was holding her cell, pointing at it with the other hand and staring at it with bulging eyes. "Olivia. That was Olivia." Nico wrapped her in a hug. She fell against his chest, breathing heavily.

"What's wrong with Olivia?"

"She was on her way out of work last night when her car exploded."

"What?" Nico exchanged a look with Xavier. "You're sure about that?"

"Should I have asked for pictures? Yes, I'm sure. It's what she said. Her car blew up. Thank God she wasn't close enough to it to be hurt badly."

"Were there any casualties otherwise?"

"No, nobody got hurt. But there was a lot of damage done to the other cars parked near hers."

Xavier thought back to the grand opening party

in Pine Cove. Olivia. She'd struck him as the group leader, almost, the strongest personality. Yet instead of turning him off the way strident, loud women tended to do, he'd sensed her kindness. She had a big heart, a lot of love for her friends.

"Why would anyone want to bomb her car? What kind of work is she in?"

"She works at a publishing house. She's an editor. She's a normal person." Right. While Xavier had never been anything remotely normal, he suspected normal, innocent humans rarely had their cars bombed.

"I need to get to her. Right away." Megan clutched Nico tightly, her eyes darting over his face. "Okay? Can we go? I don't trust myself to drive. I'm too upset."

"Of course. Whatever you need." Then, as one, they turned to Xavier, as if remembering he was there.

"You should come with us." Nico scowled as soon as Xavier began sputtering, trying to come up with an excuse. "A change of scene would do you good. And who knows? You might be able to help somehow."

How he could be of help to anyone was a mystery, but he was in no mood to get into it.

Besides, there was only so much self-pity he could take. "So long as you think it's a good idea."

"I'm sure Olivia will be glad to have as many good people around her right now as possible." Megan ran her hands through her hair, distracted. Xavier could scent her fear and panic in the sweat now beading at her temples. "Let me grab my bag and we'll go."

Xavier took the opportunity to duck inside and grab his duffel bag. Denver might be a good place to disappear, come to think of it. Obviously, staying with Nico would only end up putting a wedge between them. They'd barely sat and talked for five minutes before tensions began to rise. The last thing he wanted was to destroy lifelong friendships.

He would follow them to Denver and check in on Olivia, but that would be it. After that, he was on his own. Whether he wanted to be or not.

It was early morning by the time they arrived in Denver. Olivia's apartment building sat on the outskirts of the city, and Xavier followed Nico's truck to a parking garage attached to a tall, brick building.

From the looks of the façade, it was a historic structure. Were editors paid that well?

Megan practically ran for the elevator once they were inside, no matter how Nico reminded her Olivia wasn't in danger. Once they reached the fourth floor, she flew down the hall and banged on the door. The men winced, exchanging a look. It was pretty early to be banging on a Sunday morning.

"I'm so glad you're here." Olivia disentangled herself from Megan's tight embrace before greeting Xavier and Nico once they reached the apartment. "I swear, I feel like I'm losing my mind."

"You haven't slept, have you?" Megan touched a hand to Olivia's cheek. "Let me fix us some tea. Do you have any? I could run down to the corner if not."

"Sure, in the cabinet above the sink." Megan hurried off, leaving Olivia to drop to the sofa and draw her feet beneath her. She pulled her sleeves down over her hands, then wrapped her arms around herself. The very definition of a person trying to protect herself from the world.

Nico took a seat in an overstuffed chair to her left, angling his body toward hers. "So what happened? What led to this? Have you been receiving threats?"

Olivia shook her head, her lips pressed tight

together. "You're not going to believe this. And Meg, I'm sorry I never told you."

"Never told me what?" Megan poked her head out through the kitchen doorway.

"Who my father is. Or was." She wore a smirk, looking around the room. "I assume none of you have checked the news lately?"

They all shook their heads, shrugging.

"I never had much of a relationship with my father after my parents divorced. He met a new woman, left us and married her. What I never told anyone about was his company in Silicon Valley. A major player in the tech world. Fortune 500 level stuff."

Xavier snapped his fingers in recognition. "The CEO whose car blew up. I heard about it on the radio, in the truck."

"What?" Megan's question echoed around the apartment. "Your father was murdered?"

Olivia nodded slowly. "Around ten days ago. The funeral was this past Monday."

Megan flew to her side. "Wait a second. You never even told me your dad died. Olivia, oh my God."

She lifted a shoulder, wearing a weak smile that looked like a half-hearted apology even to someone who didn't know her. "Like I said, we had no relationship. And at the time, I didn't know how it happened. I didn't know anything about it until Friday when it was all over the news. I'm talking every outlet. And even though I never used his last name, somebody figured out I'm his daughter—and he willed me his entire estate. Including the company."

"Holy shit." Nico clasped his hands on top of his head. "It's amazing you're still functioning with all this happening at once."

"I thought I was doing okay until, you know." She made a sound with her lips like an explosion, miming one with her arms before wrapping them around herself again. "And they told me I might need a bodyguard, too, but I ignored them."

"Who are *they*?"

"My father's lawyers, from some big firm out in California. They came in to give me the papers for the will and, I don't know, I guess to transfer all his things to me. They neglected to tell me about the explosion. Now, they want to offer me protection. A bodyguard I can trust. But who is that? I mean, what do I do? Google it? Check out their Yelp reviews?" She blurted out a crazy sort of laugh. "How is this my life?"

Nico and Megan exchanged a look over the top of Olivia's head. Then, to Xavier's dismay, Nico looked his way while arching an eyebrow.

Megan, meanwhile, pleaded silently with him.

The kettle's whistle couldn't have come at a better time. Olivia got up to help Megan with the tea, giving Xavier time to tear into his friend. "It's not happening." He kept his voice low, one eye always on the kitchen.

"She needs help."

"Obviously. But not from me. And you know why."

"You'll be fine."

"Easy for you to say. You know what I'm dealing with."

"And now you know what she's dealing with. It would be good for you."

Somehow, this struck Xavier as the most ridiculous notion of all. "How so?"

"It will give you something to focus on. You said it yourself. When you were helping Drake, it gave you something to focus on. You could channel your energy into finding that maniac who was stalking Audra." When Xavier looked away, wishing he had never shared that bit of information, Nico pressed him. "Isn't that true?"

"Just because it worked then doesn't mean it's going to work again."

"Man, she needs help. She's terrified. And she's a good one, like a sister to Megan. If we weren't in the middle of our research, I would stay with her."

"Does she know about us?" No need to elaborate.

Nico shook his head, glancing toward the kitchen. "They've all kept it from her."

"What if I—"

"You won't. You controlled it in Pine Cove. You'll control it here."

So much for getting away. No matter how he protested, he knew it was the right thing to do. If he left without making sure she was safe, he would never get her out of his head. And Nico knew it, of course. There was a downside to knowing each other so well.

He could do worse—and had in the past. While the plant-filled, feminine space wasn't to his taste, it was clean and comfortable. Photos of Olivia's friends covered the walls and flat surfaces. He recognized all of the girls. She loved them fiercely. How he knew it was a mystery, but the feeling was strong.

There was another feeling, even stronger. He studied the photos, his eyes always landing on Olivia's beaming image. She drew him in. Made him wonder why she compelled his curiosity. Then again, anyone would be curious over a girl willing to refuse a fortune. That had to be the extent of it. There couldn't be more than that, not the way he was.

This was a good person stuck in an unthinkable situation. She deserved help. "Fine. Only for a few days, until she finds a permanent solution."

Any longer than that and he might find himself too wrapped up in her to leave.

And he was the last thing she needed.

4

———

Nothing like being forced to spend time with a complete stranger. Still, Megan was right. It was better than hiring somebody off the street. According to Nico, Xavier was trustworthy and never backed down from a confrontation. While that didn't bode well for their time together since she, too, rarely backed down from a fight and sometimes let her temper get away from her, it was better to have a scrapper in her corner than nobody at all.

"Can I offer you something to eat?" Yes, because that was what people said in situations like this. Painfully awkward situations. "I can only imagine you all drove through the night."

He nodded, his back to her while he gazed out

the window. "We did. I can head out and grab food." His voice was deep, like a growl.

Something inside her tightened when he said it. "No, if you don't mind. I would like it if you stayed here." She burst out laughing at herself before covering her face with her hands. "I'm sorry. I don't know what I'm doing. This is all so weird."

"For me, too, if it makes you feel any better."

"Wouldn't you know it, it doesn't." But at least he grinned over his shoulder, albeit briefly. She didn't feel so guilty for keeping him there, which she realized was where a lot of her current strain came from. "I'm sorry for this. I'm sure it's the last thing you expected. Megan said you've been traveling around and were just stopping in to visit with them when I called. You didn't sign on for babysitting duty."

"I'm glad to be here." Somehow, she sensed that wasn't entirely the truth. Megan had practically strongarmed him into it.

"I only wish I had more room for you."

"The couch is fine."

Now she was glad she'd chosen one long enough to fit his body. Like Nico, he was almost absurdly tall. Come to think of it, all of those boys from around Shotgun Falls were abnormally large, broad-shouldered, big in the chest and arms. Xavier was no exception. If she hadn't been half out of her mind with fear after watching her life flash before her eyes, this could be a very different sort of situation.

Currently, however, sex and dating and even flirting were the last things on her mind.

"How about this. I'll place an order to have something delivered for breakfast. Later, I can order groceries. Sound good?"

"I'd be happy to chip in."

"Don't even think about it. You're doing me a huge favor." She pulled up a local diner and placed an order and tried to pretend it was perfectly normal for him to ask for two stacks of pancakes and a double order of bacon.

Funny. That was the first task she'd started and actually finished since the explosion. After getting checked out at the hospital, she'd been too spaced out to concentrate on any one thing for very long.

Over their breakfast, enjoyed at the coffee table, he asked a single question out of the blue. "Why don't you want any of what your father left you?"

She nearly choked on her omelet. For somebody who barely spoke, he knew how to ask hard-hitting questions when he felt like it. "Because it's not mine. I didn't ask for it."

"He must have had a reason."

"If he did, he never shared it with me. He never shared anything with me. I figured he forgot he even had a daughter." She shrugged helplessly. "I don't know how to run a Fortune 500 company. I wouldn't know how to talk to a board of directors. I don't want the headaches that come along with maintaining vacation properties I'll probably never have time to visit. I have no intention of giving up my career just because somebody handed me a bunch of money and a ton of responsibilities."

She watched him process this, his brow furrowing, his dark eyes narrowing. He probably thought she was the world's biggest idiot, the way anybody would. But instead of asking if she needed to see a doctor, he nodded, then picked up a slice of bacon. "I'd feel the same way."

How refreshing. "In fact, I'm waiting for a decent time to call the lawyer. After what happened on Friday, I definitely want no part of any of this."

"Do you think they'll go along with it?"

"Honestly, I don't care." She looked him up and down, barely able to suppress a grin. "And if they want to meet in person, maybe the sight of you will get them to back down."

"What does that mean?"

She froze. *Terrific. He's been here for all of thirty*

minutes and you already insulted him. Way to go. "I'm just saying. You're kind of..."

He smiled. "I knew what you meant. I can be intimidating."

He was kind, if not exactly warm. She didn't need a friend at the moment. She needed a protector. If he was willing to do the job, he could be as awkward and short-spoken as he wanted.

By the end of the day, she'd settled things with the lawyers, who didn't seem so surprised anymore that she was willing to sign over everything she'd been given. "I don't care who gets it. Melanie, charity, the gardener. I'm signing it all away."

"That means control of your father's company will go to the board of directors."

"Godspeed to them. I'm sure they're much better suited to run things than I would ever be." Since they were on FaceTime, she made a point to angle the camera so Xavier was also captured in the frame. "I'm all set here with a bodyguard." Was it her imagination, or did he grunt for added effect?

"We'll email you the documents and you can sign electronically." She happily agreed to this and promised to check her email for the files. At least that was taken care of.

As the day wound down, though, with the two of

them coexisting in almost complete silence while watching TV, the sense of Monday morning looming large made her heart hammer. Nobody would blame her for taking time off, she knew that much. Her inbox was full of concerned messages, all of them wishing her well and checking to make sure she was in one piece. Was it wrong to wonder how much of that had to do with curiosity and how much came from actual concern?

It was either sit in the living room with Xavier for the foreseeable future or go to work and try to make his presence seem normal.

She cleared her throat, which was the first sound either of them had made in at least an hour. "I'm going to have to go to work tomorrow. I can't let them win, whoever they are."

He grunted in reply. Was that an affirmation? Was it too much to ask for a word rather than a sound?

"I hope that won't be too awkward for you. I'm sure nobody would question you being there. Everybody knows what happened."

"Just find me a chair to sit in." His gaze never left the TV screen. "If you see anything out of the ordinary, let me know." It was as simple as that?

One thing she knew for sure: she'd have her eyes

peeled for anything that seemed even slightly out of the ordinary. After watching her car explode in front of her and being knocked flat by the force, she wondered if she'd spend a day without looking over her shoulder or questioning everyone around her ever again.

OLIVIA QUIRKED A BROW. "Put your eyes back in your head."

Lauren jumped a little, pulling her attention from Xavier who currently was on his way to the men's room. "My eyes are just fine."

"No, they're stuck to his ass. This is me you're talking to." Granted, he looked good coming and going, but still. "The last thing he needs is all of us drooling over him."

"All of us?" Lauren's eyebrows moved up and down suggestively.

"You know what I'm saying, so don't even try it."

"Come on. I know what happened on Friday was traumatic, and I still can't understand why you would come to work today, but let's not kid ourselves." She craned her neck to look down the hall again even though by then he had to be out of sight. "The man is sex on two legs. And he's staying with you?"

"Get your mind out of the gutter. Besides, he's barely strung three sentences together since he showed up yesterday."

"Who's trying to have a conversation?"

Olivia burst out laughing. There was no helping it. And it felt good to laugh for a little while. For those few seconds, she wasn't the girl whose car got blown up. She was only herself. "Stop. You're not helping."

Lauren followed her to her desk, still breathless. "So, what, is he sleeping on the couch?"

"Of course he is, and I thought I asked you to stop. I don't need to be thinking about him that way."

"You are a stronger woman than me, that's for sure."

Olivia rolled her eyes. "What, would you fake a nightmare to get him to sleep with you?"

"Maybe. I saw it in a book once."

"You're the worst. Do me a favor, okay? Just tell everybody to kind of lay off him. He's not big on conversation as it is, and I don't want to scare him off." Lauren sketched a quick salute before hustling down the hall. Who did she think she was fooling, slowing down as she approached the men's room like she was hoping to run into Xavier?

It would be that way as long as he was around, she guessed. There were a lot of single girls in the office, not to mention a few married women who never shied away from gossiping over hot guys.

So long as none of them insulted him, it was all harmless. What worried her most was controlling her own thoughts. Daydreaming about him would be dangerous. It was bad enough she couldn't help the nervous butterflies that always seemed to awaken in her stomach whenever their eyes met.

By the time he returned, she was seated behind her desk. "I made sure they set up a little area for you over there." She nodded toward the corner, where a high-backed chair and footstool waited. She made sure to ask for the biggest, sturdiest chair in the office to accommodate his size. "We have an extensive library filled with all the books the company has published. You're more than welcome to read any of them. Or you could just, you know, do stuff on your phone."

He nodded before crossing the room and taking a seat. He moved the footstool aside before settling in, elbows propped on the armrests, hands folded in his lap.

Okay, then. That was how he wanted to play this. "Let me know if you need anything. There's lots of food and drinks in the break room, too, and everybody's free to use them."

He inclined his head as if he understood, but said nothing.

Terrific. Getting work done would be totally easy with somebody staring silently at the back of her head all day. She decided to dive headfirst into reviewing a new manuscript. If the writing was good enough, the story would suck her in and it wouldn't matter who was staring at the back of her head.

The writing wasn't good enough. Not that there was anything wrong with it, but nothing short of the next Pulitzer winner would be enough to make her forget Xavier's presence. She was keenly aware of everything: her posture, the way she tended to fidget while reading. Even the sound of her breathing, which sounded obnoxiously loud in the otherwise silent room.

She couldn't hear his breathing. Was he dead? If she looked at him, what would she find? Would he still be staring at her, or would he have the decency to look out the window, instead?

He cleared his throat, making her jump.

"Didn't mean to startle you."

It was an excuse to look his way. Even now, after having been around him for more than twenty-four hours, there was no ignoring the way her heart skipped a beat whenever she set eyes on him. She swallowed hard and hoped she wouldn't say anything embarrassing. "What's up?"

"Is this what you do all day?"

"That's part of it." She grinned before patting the stack of paper at one corner of her desk. "You interested in helping me?"

"I have enough on my mind."

"I see. I'm probably the last person you feel like hanging around."

"It's not that." He stretched his long legs out in front of him, crossing them at the ankles. "You answered my question."

What an odd duck. She turned back to the manuscript and realized she'd completely forgotten where she left off. She wasn't concentrating. How was she supposed to function? A bodyguard was bad enough, but this guy? When she wasn't reminding herself to stop checking him out, she was asking herself questions about him. Why was he so quiet? What did he do with his life that he could drop everything out of nowhere to look after her? What was he getting out of this? They had never even discussed payment. The way things stood, he was doing a favor for a friend. It seemed like a pretty big sacrifice.

One thing was for sure—she would get nowhere if she didn't buckle down and get her head in the game. She hadn't worked so hard for so long and dealt with so many condescending pricks in the publishing world to get fired over a vague threat and the hunk protecting her from it.

5

───────

I t was the growling that woke her up.

Her eyes snapped open, her body frozen in fear. At first, she didn't know what she was afraid of or why she had woken up at all—until she heard it again. A growl so clear, so menacing, it made the hair on the back of her neck stand up.

She stared at the ceiling, her breath coming in short little gasps. A dog? It was a pet-free building. There was no reason why she should hear any kind of animal, especially four floors up. This was no stray wandering around under her window.

Silence stretched out, broken only by the rapid thud of her pulse in her ears. Maybe she really had imagined it. Maybe she was still partway inside a dream. She had been dreaming about dogs, hadn't she?

No. Wolves. They were sometimes spotted on the outskirts of the city, having wandered too close to civilization. It usually meant they were hungry. They didn't want to hurt anybody. Why would she dream about them? Then she remembered it had only been a few days since seeing Nico and Megan, the wolf preservationists. Her subconscious was tying up loose ends.

She rolled onto her side, toward the window, but hadn't yet closed her eyes when a soft thud startled her again. There was no pretending it hadn't come from the living room. She threw back the covers and was halfway done putting on a robe to cover up her pajamas when a bloodcurdling thought hit her. What if somebody had broken in and Xavier was fighting them off? Did she need to show herself if that was the case?

No. If that was the case, there'd be a lot more than a single thud. That was what she told herself as she opened the bedroom door.

Dawn wasn't far away. The sky outside the windows was gray, the light coming through enough to give her a clear view of the man standing in front of them. His back was to her, his shoulders rising and falling like he had just finished an intense work-out. What was it she'd heard about him? He'd been in the military. Maybe he was used to getting up this early.

"I heard a noise out here. Is everything okay?"

For a moment, he did nothing but continue that heavy breathing. The hair stood on the back of her neck again. This time she couldn't figure out why. She was about to repeat her question when he grunted.

"Fine. Sorry for waking you."

"I would have woken up in a little while, anyway." That wasn't technically true, but it wouldn't kill her to get out of bed a little earlier than usual. She was halfway through turning back toward the bedroom when she remembered why she'd woken up in the first place. "Is it just me, or was something growling? Did you hear it? Out in the hallway, maybe?"

"No."

That was it. No questions, no comment on how weird it was that she would hear that. It must have been part of a dream, after all. Since it was clear he didn't feel like making conversation, she hurried back to her room and left him to his panting.

There was no hope of getting back to sleep, and

she would only feel like garbage later on if she did. It was amazing she could sleep at all with so many questions running through her mind no matter how she tried to quiet them down. It was impossible not to wonder about him. Who was he? Being reserved was one thing, but he turned it into an art form. She never knew how he felt about anything, what his opinion was. If he didn't mind sitting in her office for the past three days with nothing to do but watch her work, or if it drove him out of his skull. He didn't exactly seem like a man who spent his life sitting around. He had to be bored senseless.

And why did he sometimes get up out of nowhere and march down the hall? She assumed he was going to the men's room, but when he came back he always looked sort of wild. There was a strange look in his eyes, and his short, dark hair would be mussed. Sometimes he looked rumpled, too, the way he did in the living room. She hadn't thought much of it at the time, but it looked like he'd been... what? Rolling around on the floor? She was thinking too much about it.

She was still thinking about it when they reached the office later that morning—until they stepped onto the floor and found utter chaos.

"Olivia!" Lauren came tearing down the hall toward them, eyes wide and wild. "Somebody broke in overnight. Everything's a mess in your office!"

"Wait here." Xavier was already on his way down the hall before Olivia could wrap her head around what she'd heard.

"My office?" She looked around to find dozens of pairs of eyes staring at her. "Was anything else touched?"

"Everything else seems okay." Chloe's voice trembled like it was her life being thrown upside down.

Lauren leaned closer, putting an arm around her. "It only seemed to be your office."

"I'm sorry." Who was she apologizing to? And why did she feel the need to do it? None of this was her fault. She hadn't made any of this happen.

Xavier marched their way and once again, Olivia noted the strange look in his eyes. Almost like they were changing color, but then that was impossible. Her mind was playing tricks on her. "It's wrecked. I'm sorry."

"I want to see it."

"We're getting back on the elevator and getting you out of here. The cops will take care of this."

She glared up at him. "I want. To see. It."

He scowled, but stepped aside. "Go ahead." The sound of a man who knew she'd wish she'd listened.

It only set her teeth on edge. She strode down the hall with her head held high. Nobody was going to intimidate her and get away with it.

Or so she thought until she set eyes on the knife stuck in her desk. Somebody had used enough force to leave it standing straight up among the strewn papers, the broken chairs, the plants that had been unpotted and thrown around. Someone had smeared dirt from one of them on the wall, along with the words DIE BITCH in what looked like lipstick. She kept a few tubes in her desk drawer for quick touch-ups. They'd repeated the message on a piece of paper impaled on the knife.

"I want to go home." She reached out blindly and touched Xavier's arm. He took her hand without saying a word and led her from the room, down the hall, and into the elevator car. No one tried to stop them.

Once she was outside, it seemed her thoughts cleared. Maybe it was the distance she'd placed between herself and the death threat upstairs. A death threat. What had she ever done to deserve that?

The moment she was seated in Xavier's truck, she decided to find out. "Who are you calling?" She didn't answer his question. He'd find out soon enough.

When Jacob answered, she laid into him. "Now I have people breaking into my office, destroying it, and writing 'die bitch' on my wall. Are you sure there's nothing you've neglected to tell me?"

He sputtered for a second or two before murmuring something away from the microphone. When he returned, his voice was hollow. "I honestly have no idea why any of this would happen. Sincerely. Especially now that you've signed away your inheritance."

"And that's gone through? You submitted the paperwork?"

"Yes, though it might not have been processed yet. Even if it has, it's likely word hasn't gotten out."

"Is there a way we could spread the word? I'm sick of this. I can't live this way." There was a tremble in her voice and she hated it. This wasn't her. She wasn't weak and weepy. Yet the evidence proved otherwise.

Xavier's hand closed over her knee, giving her a

firm squeeze before withdrawing. It would've seemed overly familiar under any other circumstance. Now, she welcomed it.

"We'll do everything we can to spread the word. I can have a press release ready within the hour. We'll release it as soon as we run it past you."

"Don't even bother with that step. Just tell them I don't want the money or the company or any of it. I trust you with this." She ended the call before she did something embarrassing like bursting into tears. It would be one thing to do that in front of a friend, like Megan, but a stranger? Unthinkable.

She glanced at Xavier, whose attention appeared to be focused on the road. She suspected otherwise. Though there was no reason for it, she had the sense of understanding certain things about him. Like the way he only pretended not to pay attention sometimes. His rigid posture told another story. Of all the mysteries wrapped around him, that was the one she'd cracked. Not exactly helpful.

Stepping into the apartment brought only one thought to mind, and it wasn't safety. "I'm exhausted." She kicked off her heels and wished he wasn't around so she could take off her bra then and there without having to worry about modesty. It was definitely a 'remove the bra the second the door's locked' kind of day.

"I'd be worried about you if you weren't. You've had a lot happen in a short time."

It was almost as much as he'd ever said to her at one time, and he didn't sound as growly as usual. She took it as a good sign, but her conscience plagued her nonetheless. "And I dragged you into it. I should be looking for another bodyguard so you can get back to your life."

He grunted, shaking his head. "I'm here for the long haul. Try to get some rest."

His eyes met hers, but instead of the usual butterflies, she only felt warmth. Comfort. "Thank you. Could I ask another favor?"

His lips twitched. "What?"

"Would you mind if I hung out with you instead of going to my room?" She rubbed her arms, lowering her gaze. It had never been easy to admit needing anyone or anything. "I would rather not be alone. And I could use a little mindless TV."

"It's your home. I'll keep an eye on you." By the time she emerged from her room wearing a t-shirt and sweats, he'd made up the couch the way he did for himself every night. She murmured her thanks before settling in, then promptly fell asleep. There was no fighting it. The weight of everything going on was too draining.

It felt like she had only closed her eyes for a second before something touched her face.

Not something. Someone.

Someone hovering close. Someone whose hand covered her mouth, fingers pressed into her cheek.

Panic made her struggle weakly for a moment before she realized it was Xavier. Darkness was starting to fall and the lights were now on. She'd slept through the day. And for some reason, he was now on one knee, covering her mouth while glaring at the front door.

When the doorknob jiggled, she understood why.

Someone was trying to break in.

With Olivia pinned under him, he assessed the situation.

There was no way out of the apartment now. No fire escape. He doubted this was a run-of-the-mill robbery attempt. They'd be on a mission, whoever they were. His only objective was keeping her safe, which meant pulling her up from the sofa and rushing her to her room.

Once they were there, he held a finger to his lips before whispering. "Stay here until I come for you. Don't open the door for anything." The last thing he saw was her wide, fearful eyes before closing the door as quietly as he could manage.

He turned out the lights in the living room, plunging the apartment into darkness. The light from the hall leaked in from under the door. He watched, holding his breath while shadows moved out there. Two people, at least.

Two people, probably men, sent to attack and maybe kill a defenseless woman.

Little did they know she wasn't alone. Anger began to rise in him just as the lock disengaged and the door swung open. Two men stormed in, dressed in black, and stopped short when they found the place dark.

Dark enough to miss the presence of the man waiting behind the door.

He took the first one out easily, using the side of his hand in a chopping motion against the back of his neck hard enough to knock him out. The second of the men swung around while reaching for something in his pocket. A gun? He didn't have time to reach it before Xavier grabbed him in a headlock, cutting off his oxygen. It wasn't long before the man went limp.

What to use to tie them up? He went through the kitchen drawers and came up with a roll of duct tape. There was more than enough for the two of them. Once they were secured, he planned on questioning both. Or perhaps one at a time while the other watched. It had been a long time since he'd used the techniques learned during his time in the military, but those skills weren't the sort a person forgot.

Before the end of the night, he'd have answers. The thought alone was enough to make him smile to himself as he wrapped layers of tape around the intruders' ankles and wrists. It would be fun watching them wake up, observing as understanding dawned on them. They had been sent to kill a girl who'd never hurt anyone and were about to wake up at the mercy of a—

No. No, not now.

He straightened up, panting heavily. *Not now. Please.*

The shift was about to take over. His wolf's consciousness rose to the surface the way it had countless times during his years. Only he'd been able to control it for most of those years. It had been his choice to shift, when and where he chose to do so.

Now, it rushed up inside him with no hope of controlling it.

The worst part? How much he enjoyed it. He enjoyed the rage coursing through him, intensifying with every beat of his heart. He welcomed it, waited for it to consume him. It was always going to end this way. He was always going to have to tear them to pieces.

What little part of his human consciousness was still aware of the situation struggled desperately to regain a foothold, but it was no use. There would be no mercy for these cretins.

"Xavier?" The soft sound of Olivia's footsteps found its way into his awareness and nearly stopped his heart.

No! He turned to her, ready to beg her to run, but it was too late. It had already begun. The wolf didn't care if she watched, not when he was like this.

The shift took hold all at once, forcing him to his knees. It always hurt, though the pain was brief. The elongating of his bones and muscles, the stretching of tendons. He gritted his teeth against a howl as his skull rearranged itself and his ears repositioned. Fangs descended. Claws emerged from what were now paws.

It took no longer than a few moments for him to complete the shift. Now he looked up at her from across the room. A low growl rumbled in his throat as the wolf assessed its prey.

Back off, back off. He watched through his wolf's eyes as they approached her, one slow step at a time. She was frozen in place. Her bulging eyes and the lack of color on her skin spoke to the level of shock she was under. His human consciousness fought against it but there was no use. The wolf growled again, continuing his menacing approach. Hot, boiling rage coursed through him. *Kill. Tear. Destroy.*

Olivia remained where she was, staring at him. He came closer. She didn't move. *Run, go!* She couldn't hear him. If she could she might not be able to control her body, too horrified to move.

"Son of a bitch."

Even the wolf was surprised by this reaction. He stopped, watching her, breathing heavily. Xavier watched from behind his eyes, fighting to regain control but without success. Every muscle in his body was tensed, ready to spring.

She folded her arms and looked him up and down. "You know, like I haven't been through enough already. Father murdered. Car blown up. Office ransacked. Two guys busting into my apartment. Now I have to deal with this?"

She threw her hands into the air. "You'd think they would've told me, but nooo. They had to keep everything a big secret. I feel like such an idiot. I should've known there was something different about you guys. I mean, nobody has genes like that. They must know, right? Of course, they do. They live with these men. There's no keeping it under wraps. You lasted all of three days before showing me who you are."

An uneven laugh bubbled from her lips. "What next? Are you going to attack me? You might as well. The cherry on top of the whole situation. Just do me a favor if you can hear me in there. Make it quick."

All the while, there was nothing to do but watch and listen as she rambled on. The rage faded slowly, allowing more of Xavier's consciousness to come through the longer she spoke. She was on the verge of a breakdown. Anyone could see it. Concern over that was enough to calm him, until finally the urge to destroy her was nothing but a memory.

He was in control again. And no one had gotten hurt.

The moment he could, he shifted back, leaving him standing in front of her as a man once again. She barely registered the shift, still muttering to herself. She'd gone back to her friends and how irritated she was with them for keeping all of this a secret.

Finally, there was nothing to do but try to snap her out of it. "Olivia."

Her lashes fluttered. She shook herself slightly. "Yes. That's my name."

He waited, still watching closely for any sign of her going off the rails. "Are you... Do you need..."

She took a deep breath. "Should I call the cops now or what?"

It was his turn to blink rapidly. Who was this woman? He'd almost forgotten about the men still unconscious behind him. Somehow she had snapped straight back into the situation while he stood there, gaping at her. Shouldn't their positions be reversed?

"Well? What's the move here?" She looked around him, scowling at the sight of the men. "Are you going to question them, or are we turning them over to the cops? Whatever you think is best."

He stammered, almost at a loss. The only thing that helped was reminding himself of what was at stake. And how things could have gone if he hadn't been there.

"I was going to question them myself, but it might be better to bring the police in, instead." There was no telling whether he'd be able to control himself once he started dealing with them again. It had been so easy to slip into a rage. Why take the chance?

Olivia nodded firmly before crossing the room, stepping over one of the prone bodies on her way to the coffee table. Her phone waited there. She picked it up, dialed 911, and was calm as Xavier had ever seen anyone. "Two men broke into my apartment. They're currently unconscious and tied up. Please come as soon as you can." She rattled off the address while Xavier watched, stunned. Her voice didn't carry the flat, empty tone of someone in shock. She almost seemed to take it well. And she hadn't so much as whimpered while facing off with his wolf.

Now he knew he wasn't imagining things. There was something special about her.

And he'd come within moments of killing her.

7

———

"So then Xavier took me to my room and told me to wait in there for him. I don't know exactly how he took them down, but it didn't take long." Olivia sipped tea without tasting it or even registering the heat coming from the mug between her hands. Nothing mattered as much as keeping herself together. If she let her concentration falter for a split second, she might fall to pieces in front of a half-dozen cops.

No, there was no way of knowing exactly what would happen. She felt it, though, down deep in her core. If she took a second to think about what she'd seen, that would be it. She would start drooling on herself. Her brain would go bye-bye.

Maybe it already had, if she was thinking along these lines.

The officer in front of her made a note. "Have you ever seen either of them before?"

She craned her neck to look around the man between them. Both intruders were seated on her couch, still woozy from whatever Xavier had done to knock them out. They mumbled incoherently when questioned, while Xavier stood in the corner with another cop who asked questions in rapid succession. He handled the whole thing well, staying calm, replying in a straightforward manner.

"No. I've never set eyes on either of them." She lifted a shoulder before taking another sip of tea. She didn't even want it, but she had to do something with her hands, and holding a mug was as good as anything else.

"And you believe this is tied to Marcus Pemberton's death?"

Was the man hearing impaired or just ignorant? The question came dangerously close to tumbling from her lips, but she stopped it in time. "I can't imagine what else it has to do with. His car exploded. My car exploded. My office was vandalized—they must've filed a report on that yesterday."

"Yes, we have that report on file. You never gave a statement."

The mug shook. Good thing it wasn't filled to the brim, or else she might've scalded herself. "Are you implying something? Because nobody ever called to request a statement. Considering my office was trashed and there were at least two death threats left behind, I thought it might be best to go back home. Which is what I did."

The officer's brows knitted together. "I'm sorry, Miss Barnes. That came out wrong. No one thinks you had anything to do with this."

"I would hope not. I have better things to do than blow up my car and vandalize my workspace." She forced herself to take a deep breath, though it did nothing to ease the tension in her head. "Before his death, nothing like this had ever happened to me. I live a quiet life. I don't even date much, if at all."

Too much information? Maybe not. They might ask if she had any angry exes, at least until they could get a straight answer out of the blubbering goons on the couch. Once they came to fully, they might give details of who'd hired them and why. Not to mention what the endgame of tonight's break-in was supposed to be.

Last night's break-in, actually. The clock over the

stove read 12:30. They'd been at this for hours already, with cops taking pictures of the crime scene —though there wasn't much to photograph, since Xavier had taken care of them so fast. There wasn't time to do more than break the lock on the front door. Since then, they'd answered countless questions, sometimes twice or even three times by as many officers.

Instinct told her what that was about. They wanted to be sure there weren't any inaccuracies between one account and another. Like she had anything to lie about. Hell, Xavier had left both men with nothing but confusion and tape burn. What did he have to hide?

He had plenty to hide, and now she knew about it.

No. Later. This isn't the time. If she allowed it, she might start remembering what it was like to watch him change into a wolf. The biggest wolf she'd ever seen. His fur was the same dark brown as Xavier's hair and his eyes had glowed with a swirling, amber light.

He was beautiful. He was also angry. Very. She'd felt it in her bones and heard it in the way he'd growled. The way he'd advanced on her like he was hungry, and she was his next meal.

But she hadn't been afraid. She still wasn't. It seemed strange. Shouldn't she have screamed? Shouldn't she still be screaming? The thought of telling the cops about him hadn't even entered her mind. Why not? Right, because they'd lock her up for at least seventy-two hours to make sure she wasn't a danger to herself or others. Nobody would believe it without seeing it.

She'd seen it and hardly believed it herself.

"Thank you, Miss Barnes. We'll be in touch once we learn more about your unwanted guests here." The officer nodded toward Xavier, who was shaking hands with a pair of cops. "You're lucky you had him with you. One of those guys was carrying a gun."

It didn't come as a surprise, but an icy shiver ran down her spine anyway. She murmured her thanks and escorted everyone to the door, glad to close it behind them even if she couldn't lock it now. The locksmith would have to come in the morning. Amazing how the world kept turning after something like this.

After so much commotion, the silence left behind was deafening. She leaned against the closed door, sighing. "So that's what it feels like to call 911 because somebody broke into your apartment while carrying a gun. I can cross that one off my bucket list."

It was a joke, if a bad one, but he didn't react. "It's not safe to stay here."

"Well, yeah, without a working lock."

"You know that isn't what I mean." She flinched at the harshness behind his words. He scowled. "I'm not trying to make jokes now. You can't stay here. They know where you live and believe me, they'll send someone else once they know this first attempt failed. Next time, they won't stop at two. Not if they hear you have a bodyguard with you."

She stared at him, startled into losing her voice for a second. When his eyes narrowed, she shook herself out of her daze. "Sorry. It's just that I've never heard you string that many sentences together at once."

He shook his head. "If this is your way of coping, so be it."

"What do you want me to do? Dissolve into tears and flop around on the floor?" Only when his jaw twitched did she remember who she was dealing with. And what she had seen him do. Was it a good idea to antagonize a man who could shift into a wolf? "Sorry. It's been—"

"I know. You don't have to apologize."

"So if I'm not safe here, where are we going?"

"I'm going to settle that right now, while you go in and pack." She had her marching orders, then. It would be a good idea to do as he asked without arguing. Besides, she trusted him. Despite everything she'd seen, the one thing she knew was he'd never hurt her. Not even when there was nothing stopping him, like earlier. He could've torn her to pieces with those fangs of his. Strange how the memory didn't scare her. Unnerved, sure, but she wasn't afraid.

Before packing, she washed the mug and left it to dry on the counter. Who knew when they'd be back?

Not the best question to ask herself, since thinking of leaving her beloved home only brought tears to her eyes. She had worked so hard, and for what? To let somebody take it away? There was no way to fight it, either. Stubbornness wouldn't get her anywhere, not now.

How long a trip was she packing for? While she didn't want to believe she'd be gone more than a few days, her practical side won out. Better to pack for at least a week, and if she needed to, she could always find a laundromat. With no idea where they were going, she had to consider all possibilities. Jeans, t-shirts, a few thin sweaters in case they ended up at a higher elevation, plus it could still get cold at night. Hiking boots, tennis shoes. She emptied out most of her lingerie and socks, cramming them into a smaller bag along with toiletries and makeup. Even now, she was packing makeup. Her life was in danger and somehow, she needed mascara.

The lock on the door was broken, meaning anybody could come in. She texted the property manager to explain as vaguely as possible that she had to go out of town and the apartment would be unlocked until the door was fixed, then packed a few pieces of jewelry handed down through the years, just in case. That and her MacBook seemed like the only things she couldn't easily replace. Even her photos were all stored digitally, though she couldn't imagine why anybody would want them.

Even all this last-minute panic wasn't enough to distract her from the very real, very dangerous wolf she'd seen earlier. Now that she knew the truth, she saw so much through different eyes. All the little things about the guys her friends had paired up with. Like the way the girls always had to move their lives to where their men were. It struck her as odd at the time, like when Charlotte and Hope both moved to Shotgun Falls permanently and virtually abandoned the lives they'd lived before that. No wonder it had to be that way. Otherwise, it would mean wolf shifters living away from... what? Their pack? It explained their size, for sure. And why, whenever she'd asked questions about what the guys did for a living or where they went to school—normal questions, the kind people always asked—she never got answers. The best she'd ever received were half-answers quickly followed up by a change in subject.

It was all so obvious, but that was how hindsight worked. If they didn't think they were going to get an earful from her once things calmed down, they had another think coming.

She was zipping up her suitcase when Xavier knocked on the bedroom door. "You almost ready?"

"Just about. Where are we going?"

"Pine Cove. I just got off the phone with Drake. Tourist season doesn't start for another few weeks so they're empty at the moment. It makes the most sense for us to stay there."

"That works for me." Not that she had much of a choice in the matter. At least she would be able to tear into Audra about keeping secrets.

She took one more look around her apartment after checking to make sure everything was turned off and safe. Her plants would go unwatered. Of all the things to feel bad about at a time like this. She forced herself through the door and hoped it wouldn't be the last time she ever set eyes on the place.

Xavier held no such affections. He was already halfway down the hall with her bags, forcing her to jog if she hoped to catch up. "Are we ever going to talk about what I saw earlier?"

"Is now the time?"

"No, but I would like to. That's not the kind of thing I can ignore. I hope you get that."

"Of course. Later."

She knew better than to ask when later would be. He'd only grunt in response. She was amazed he was actually speaking as it was.

The second they were outside on the way to his truck, she started trembling. This wasn't like her. But it wasn't like her to have men randomly breaking into her apartment, either. There was no shaking the sense of having a target painted on her back. Though it was the middle of the night and there was little foot traffic on the sidewalks, she stayed close to him. He noticed, lifting one arm slightly in a silent invitation. She wound her arms around his and held on tight as they trotted to the parking garage.

She was only able to breathe easier once she was inside the truck, with Xavier beside her. Now it was obvious he was exactly what she needed. She had seen what he could do, the way he took care of those two goons without breaking a sweat. She hadn't even heard a struggle, and nothing in the living room had been overturned. He was more than a tower of muscle. He had skills.

And he wore an expression that would have chilled her blood if they were meeting on the street. He had himself under control, but there was a definite current of anger running through him. Over her? She guessed it had to be, though she wouldn't have blamed him if he was angry on his own behalf. What should've been a couple of days had turned into something much bigger.

But it wasn't her fault. She told herself this as she made herself comfortable, using the hood of her sweatshirt as a pillow behind her neck. "I slept all day, and I'm still exhausted."

"Stress will do that." He eyed her before pulling out of the garage. "Try to get some rest. It's a long drive to Pine Cove."

He was right. Sleep would be the best thing. No sooner had she made the decision than her eyes closed and the promise of what would hopefully be sweet dreams lulled her to sleep.

8

———

After spending a few days in Denver, rolling into Pine Cove felt a lot like rolling into another world. A quieter one, peaceful, so still and silent he almost regretted breaking the peace with the sound of his truck. It was early morning when they arrived, and by the time he reached the main thoroughfare running through the heart of the commercial district, he found the grocer unrolling the awning in front of his store. There were a few vaguely familiar faces passing on the street, all of whom eyed his truck with curiosity. It wasn't often outsiders passed through at this time of year, according to Drake. If they did, they rarely stopped for more than a bite to eat and a bathroom break before continuing on.

He didn't take the curiosity for any more than what it was. They were a close-knit community, and with good reason. Shifters weren't the only supernatural creatures existing in the town. There were witches, as well, living quietly, bothering no one. Still, if word ever got out and outside humans learned of their existence, there was no telling how things might blow up. It seemed in the twenty-first century, there was still a painful amount of superstition in existence.

Olivia began to stir once he turned down the gravel road leading up to the inn. "We're here."

The fact that she'd slept through the ride was surprising. Even bumps in the road hadn't disturbed her. Nobody would know, looking in from the outside, that she was under so much stress. She had a way of pushing through that struck him as noble. Inside, though, it was clear she was crumbling. Hence the amount of sleep she'd gotten over the past twenty-four hours. Her subconscious mind wanted to retreat.

She sat up, groaning her way through a stretch. "Did I seriously sleep that long?"

"You needed it." For his part, he needed to think without her asking countless questions he was in no mood to answer. What mattered more than anything was getting to the bottom of this, and fast. Whoever was behind this wouldn't stop until they got what they wanted—or until they were put out of commission. One or the other.

"My whole body is one tight muscle." She rolled her head back and forth, wincing.

"Nothing a hot bath won't help." He tapped the horn once on pulling to a stop in front of the sprawling inn, and a moment later the screen door opened. Audra was the first onto the porch. She ran down the steps and flung Olivia's door open.

"Oh, sweetie. I'm so glad you're okay." As soon as Olivia was out of the truck, her friend enveloped her in a tight hug. At least she had good people in her corner, friends who loved her and weren't afraid to show it.

Olivia, on the other hand, seemed to be in no mood for affection. "You could have told me, you know."

Audra fell back, eyes wide. "Told you?" She exchanged a look with Drake, who now jogged down the wide steps to greet them.

"You know what I'm talking about." Olivia nodded to Drake, who lifted a hand in greeting. "Is he one of them, too? I'm sure he is. Thanks for never telling me about this."

Drake shot Xavier a questioning look. "I told you. I can't always control when it happens."

"Oh, hell." Drake ran a hand over his blonde hair, letting out a heavy sigh. "Not the best way to find out."

Audra threw her hands into the air. "I'm sorry. What was I supposed to do? This isn't the kind of thing you have a group chat about. Hey, guess what? My boyfriend can turn into a wolf."

"Fiancé." Drake shrugged when the three of them looked at him. "I'm just saying."

"They keep it secret for a reason." Audra reached for Olivia, who didn't pull away. She rubbed her arms, looking mournful. "You don't think we all wanted to tell you? I didn't know about him until way after we met, for what it's worth. It's not really something they like to lead off with when they first meet a girl, or anybody at all. It's dangerous."

Olivia was many things, but stupid wasn't one of them. Xavier watched the fight drain out of her all at once. "You're right. That was dumb of me. You know I hate being the last to know about things."

"I'm sorry. I promise, no more secrets." Audra draped an arm around her shoulders. "Come on. I fixed a big breakfast. You must be hungry. Xavier said you slept most of yesterday, so I assumed you haven't eaten."

"What else did Xavier find it his business to share?" Olivia raised an eyebrow as she passed him. There was no winning with this woman.

"I was only describing to Drake how things started last night. You were sleeping, you know." They were already inside the house, the screen door banging behind them. He turned to Drake, growling low. "The attitude on her."

"You know she's going through hell right now." Drake took Olivia's bags from the back of the truck. "Come on. I'm starving, too. You can give me the rundown over breakfast."

"You know, I still can't believe you managed to put all this together." Xavier couldn't help but admire the inn's beautiful interior, the restored trim, the shining hardwood floors. By the time he'd shown up in Pine Cove during Audra's troubles, the structure had still been in a general state of disrepair. The two of them had already done a lot of work, along with hired contractors and a cleaning crew, but this result was beyond even what Xavier had hoped his friend could achieve. He had no doubt that once tourist season came around, they would be booked solid.

As if reading his mind, Drake nodded toward the front desk. "We already have reservations through September. First guests should arrive in a couple of weeks."

"You ready for that?"

"I have to be, don't I?" He looked absurdly happy, though, which was better than many people were ever able to find for themselves.

A large part of the reason for his happiness scurried around the kitchen, her long ponytail swinging behind her. "There's coffee, tea up in the cabinet, juice. I made pancakes, eggs, bacon, sausage, and hash browns." The aroma of so much food hit Xavier like a speeding train, making his stomach growl in anticipation.

"I can't believe you went to all this trouble." Olivia took a seat near the window, holding a mug of steaming coffee. "I feel so bad, putting you out. I know you have a lot to get ready for."

"Oh, would you shut up already?" Audra said it with a smile, though, and chuckled when Olivia rolled her eyes. "Friends do this for each other. But don't get any weird ideas, either. I plan on putting you to work."

"Lucky me." Xavier wasn't fooled. He noticed the secret little smile she wore when she looked down at her mug.

Once they fixed plates for themselves, the four of them settled in around the table. Drake cleared his throat, lifting his silverware. "As much as I hate to dive right in, exactly what's happening? Xavier didn't have much time to get into it last night."

He exchanged a look with Olivia, who swallowed a mouthful of eggs before speaking. "Long story short, it seems like somebody wants me dead."

"Wow. Usually, a person has to know you before they want you dead." Olivia shot Audra a sharp look, and Audra shrank back in her chair. "I'm sorry. Now's not the time."

When Olivia looked down at her plate, now shuffling food around with her fork, Xavier took pity on her. "Last night, two men broke into the apartment. I was able to quickly incapacitate them. One of them was carrying a gun"

"With the intent to kill?"

Xavier lowered his brow at Drake, who had the decency to look embarrassed at the way he'd blurted it out. Somewhere along the way, he'd become keenly aware of Olivia's reactions, and how it might affect her to hear something like that.

"The police weren't able to get answers from them at the apartment. They were both too fuzzy to give a straight answer, though that could easily have been an act."

Drake wore an apologetic expression when he looked at Olivia. "I doubt they only wanted to scare you."

She rolled her shoulders back, cutting into a pancake with more force than was necessary. "I figured." Drake's brow furrowed, and Xavier could understand why. It was almost unnatural, watching her take this so well. Xavier knew it was an act, or maybe self-preservation. If she started thinking, really sinking into the situation and exploring what it all meant, she would collapse under the weight of it all.

"But why you? That's what I don't understand." Audra looked around the table. "I know about your dad, by the way. Megan told us all. I hope you don't mind."

"Honestly, if I could think straight right now, I would have done it myself. It's all been such a mess. I hope you don't take it personally."

"Of course not."

Xavier drained his coffee cup. It had been a very long night and he needed all the help he could get. "We can only assume it has to do with him. Especially since his killers use the same method on Olivia as they did on Mr. Pemberton."

"The car explosion." Audra went pale a moment before her chin started to quiver. Drake reached over and rubbed her leg. "I'm sorry. I know this isn't about me, but I can't help feeling like this. We could have lost you."

"But you didn't." Olivia winked and tried to smile, but it came out as more of a grimace.

"And he left everything to you. I read about that in the news." Drake got up to grab the coffee pot, topping off anyone who needed a refill.

Olivia held out her mug. "I signed it over. All of it. I don't want it."

"I saw that on the news, too. Last night. The pundits couldn't believe you would do that, in case you're curious."

"I'm just glad none of them reached out for a comment." A wicked smile tugged at the corners of her lips. "Though now I'm sorry I didn't get a chance to tell them exactly what I think about the whole situation."

"It wasn't enough for whoever's behind this to call off their dogs." Audra rested her chin on her palm. "What could they want?" Drake and Xavier exchanged a look before turning to Olivia.

Her eyes darted around the table. "How would I know? Ask Audra. We had no relationship whatsoever."

Drake didn't appear convinced. "There was never any hint that he might be involved in something he shouldn't have been?"

There it was. A momentary flash of understanding swept over her face, gone quicker than a lightning strike. "There's only one thing I can remember. Back when my parents were on the verge of their divorce, right before Dad packed up and left, I woke up one night and heard them fighting. Not that their flights were anything new. But this one, I don't know, was different."

"How so?"

"They weren't screaming. Mom wasn't throwing things or anything. Their voices were raised loud enough for me to hear, but that was it. I went to my door and opened it a little so I could hear better. I think that was the night he finally announced he was seeing somebody else. Mom made a comment about whether he thought it was wise to leave her this way when she knew so many things he wouldn't like other people knowing."

"Did she say what kind of things?"

"No, and she didn't have to. He threatened to kill

her if she ever opened her mouth. That was enough for her, I guess."

A hush went over the table. Audra chewed her lip, glancing at Drake. Xavier was too busy hating Marcus Pemberton to feel sorry for the little girl who'd heard such terrible things.

Drake cleared his throat. "That doesn't sound like the kind of thing an innocent man says to his soon-to-be ex-wife."

"I never really thought too much about it. I guess I didn't want to." Olivia set down her utensils in favor of wrapping her arms around herself. "That's not the kind of thing you want to remember. But I can't run away from these memories, because they might be sort of the answer to everything, right?"

Drake stroked his beard, grunting. "I suppose we don't have to look too hard to find a motive, then. I hate to say it, but in a situation like this, it's easy to assume the victim sort of brought it on themselves. Normal, honest people don't get their cars blown up."

"Unless they're me, remember?" Olivia waved a hand. "I didn't do anything."

"Of course, honey. That's not what he meant." While he couldn't see it under the table, there was no missing the way Audra kicked Drake.

He played it off well. "Of course, it isn't. You know I didn't mean to imply anything."

Olivia only waved her hand again, this time a dismissive gesture. "I know. Don't worry. I only wish I knew more. Names, what have you."

"As uncomfortable as it is to bring this up, maybe you could ask your mother?"

She snorted, her eyes widening. "That's the funny thing about them. Even though he left her and basically stomped on her heart, she never said a bad word about him. She's still in love with him. I wonder if I could get her to admit anything, or if she would feel disloyal or something. But I could try, for sure."

"Hopefully knowing it could save her daughter's life will be enough to get her talking."

Audra and Olivia exchanged a look. "You've never met her mom." Audra grimaced and Olivia merely nodded in agreement.

"That bad?"

"Let's just say she's never been the maternal type. But I think I might be able to get through to her. I just don't have it in me today. I need to unplug for a little bit."

"That's understandable." Drake pushed back from the table, then picked up his empty plate. "For now, I can poke around and see if anything comes up."

Olivia lifted an eyebrow. "How would you do that?"

"Some things are best left unanswered." Audra gave her friend a meaningful look. "He has his ways. In the meantime, I can take you up to your rooms. Xavier, I'm sure you'll be glad to sleep in a bed again." He couldn't pretend he wasn't looking forward to the prospect.

Drake cleared the table while Audra led them up the grand staircase. The girls walked ahead, chattering amiably about everything they wanted to do together. He could almost feel Olivia's spirits lifting and was glad he'd thought to call Drake. She needed this.

Which she didn't need, but neither of them needed, where adjoining rooms. "I figured this would be the easiest way to go about it. This way, Liv, if you need anything, Xavier's right here next door. Drake and I will be in our living quarters, but that's all the way at the other end of the hall." She pointed in that direction.

Xavier retreated to his room, which was much more feminine than anywhere he'd ever stayed. At least he'd have privacy, and somewhere to store his clothes. He unpacked, filling two dresser drawers and part of the closet. By the time he finished, Drake joined him.

Now they could speak more openly, away from the women. "It's obvious this guy had some pretty bad people in his life."

"I wish she had told me about that before." Xavier shook his head. "I mean, I understand it. She's had so many things thrown at her all at once."

"She seems to be handling it well." He jerked his chin at Xavier, cocking an eyebrow. "And she didn't run screaming, did she? Though I did catch her studying you during breakfast when you weren't looking."

"I know she has a million questions. I don't know if I can get through answering them without..." He couldn't bring himself to say it. "I can't shake the feeling that things could have gone much worse. And next time, I might not be able to hold him back."

"But you did, which means it's possible."

"You know what, maybe this isn't what I need to be doing right now." Suddenly, it was all too ridiculous. Staying at the inn, unpacking, getting settled. "I shouldn't be here. You should handle this. I can't."

"So you're going to throw this in my lap?"

"It was thrown into mine."

Drake folded his arms, planting his feet at shoulder width. "I've never seen you back down from a challenge. Not once, not ever. What's so different now?"

"You know what's different now. I don't trust myself around her. And I sure as hell don't need an adjoining room to make it that much easier for the wolf to get to her if he wants to."

"You know that's not going to happen."

"It almost did."

"Because you were enraged by the two men who broke in. Anyone would be. You're naturally protective, the way we all are. Here, things will be quieter. She'll be safe. Nobody could possibly know she's here. You can relax a little."

Xavier snorted. "I won't be able to relax until I'm away from her."

The squeak of floorboards down the hall made his head snap up. He could smell her, the fake coconut-scented shampoo she used. He crossed the room in three long strides and leaned out into the hall in time to see her disappear down the stairs. She'd been listening.

9

It was easy to see why Audra loved Pine Cove so much, especially the inn. The word *idyllic* barely began to describe how beautiful and peaceful it was when she stepped out into the garden the morning after their arrival. Butterflies floated over the daffodils and tulips that were beginning to bloom in the soft, spring sunshine. There were so many birds, their song filling the morning air and making her smile. From this vantage point, she could see the entire town laid out in front of her. The sawmill, the lake off in the distance. No wonder people flocked there in the late spring and summer. And to think, Audra would get to live there all the time.

It seemed almost too perfect.

Naturally, that meant she'd have to spoil it by calling her mother. Better to get it over with quickly. Like ripping off a Band-Aid.

"It's a little early in the morning, isn't it?"

She rolled her eyes. "Good morning to you, too, Mom."

"It must be something pretty important if it means calling me. I'm usually the one who has to hunt you down."

Gee, I wonder why? "Who wouldn't want to call and hear this first thing in the morning? Yes, it is pretty important."

"What's the matter?"

Nobody would believe it unless they knew the woman. Anyone who'd never met her would think there had to be something wrong with Olivia for not having told her mom about any of the threats she'd received. She couldn't even pretend it was a means of sparing her mother's blood pressure, either. The woman always found a way to turn everything into a problem for her.

She didn't mince words, giving her mother a breakdown of what had been happening. She didn't tell her where she was or that she'd ever left Denver —not that she didn't trust her, but she was afraid of a surprise visit. Nobody needed that.

"So that's it. I'm safe right now, no need to worry. But I thought I would let you know."

"Has it ever occurred to you to warn me, in case someone wanted to come after me, too?"

And there it was. "Just once, Mom, I wish you would surprise me. No, it didn't occur to me, because I figured you would tell me the second you received anything close to a threat. And you aren't the one he willed everything to. Why would anybody have a problem with you?"

"Have all the transfers going through? I assume the lawyers took care of everything."

Olivia's mouth fell open. "Mom. You're not listening to me. I didn't take anything. There was a press release about that. I don't want any of it."

"So you would turn down a fortune like that? All because of some silly, ancient grunge?"

"Mom, are you even hearing me? I just finished telling you somebody tried to kill me more than once in the past week, and all you care about is my refusing the inheritance. It was my call, not yours."

"I can't believe you. What goes through your head?"

"I could ask you the same question. It's good to know you care so much." She ended the call and barely stopped short of throwing the phone across the garden. How could the two of them be related? The woman lived in a fantasy world. So much for getting any information out of her, but even an angel would curse until they were blue in the face after spending thirty seconds arguing with somebody who always seemed to be having a completely different conversation.

The hair on the back of her neck rose, and she went still. He was watching. She always felt when he was nearby. "Are you going to come out here, or are you going to hang out on the porch?"

It took him a second to answer. "I'll stay here."

She turned, throwing her arms wide. "I'm not going to bite you." He flinched slightly and she wished she hadn't said it. "I'm sorry. I didn't mean that the way it sounded."

"It's fine."

"Could you at least come out here? I was enjoying looking at the flowers, and I don't like having to shout at you." He glowered at her but started for the stairs. That was all it took to get him to listen?

Still, he kept his distance, hands shoved in his pockets. "Seriously? Do I have a disease you don't want to catch?" When all he did was grunt and turn his back on her, she marched over to him and tapped him on the shoulder. "See? Not so scary."

"Says you."

"Oh, so I'm the scary one? Is that what you're telling me? And is that why you tried to get Drake to take over for you so you could sneak out?" It still stung a day later, hearing that. No, she shouldn't have been listening. Still. Why did he have to say it?

"Don't push me."

"I didn't know I was pushing. I only thought I was trying to get answers."

He tipped his head back, growling up at the sky. "Maybe not everything needs an answer. You can't bulldoze your way through everything."

"That's what you think of me? That I bulldoze my way through things? If I did, I'd have the slightest clue who you are or what you're about. But all you do is grunt and growl."

"Maybe you should take that as a hint."

"Maybe you should stop being so freaking impossible. I'm not afraid of you if that's what you think. This isn't some false show of bravado or whatever. But I like you as a person, and I hate the feeling that you're pushing me away. Am I that bad? Are you that desperate to get rid of me?"

"That's not what this is about. I wish you would at least try to understand."

"Then what is it about? How would I know if you never tell me?"

There it was. A sudden change in the air. An electrical charge, or what felt like one. Almost as if a thunderstorm was on its way.

His breathing picked up. He started panting like he did the morning she woke up to the sound of growling. Now she knew it was him doing the growling.

Still, it didn't scare her. Why didn't it scare her? "Why can't you talk to me?"

"Back off. I'm warning you."

"Why? I'm not going to tell anybody if that's what you're worried about." She reached out again, this time wanting nothing more than to put a hand on his shoulder so he knew she was trying to be a friend.

Yet the second she made contact, he spun around, his eyes glowing with that amber light she'd seen at the apartment. "I said, back off." His voice didn't sound like his anymore—deeper, animal, menacing. "Go in the house. Now."

"I'm not afraid." She planted her feet, lifting her chin. "You don't scare me."

Yet when his chest started to heave and his face went red, she started having second thoughts. By the time she began backing away, it was too late. The shift had already started.

In some ways, it was beautiful. Light surrounded him in a halo a moment before his skin started to ripple. He fell on his hands and knees, growling louder than before. His skeleton seemed to rearrange itself, lengthening, fur sprouting up over the length of him.

It didn't take long. The time it took her heart to beat a few furious times. Suddenly she was faced with the same enormous, muscular, growling wolf as she'd faced in the apartment.

And he had his eyes locked on her.

"I'm not afraid." He growled in response, taking a step closer. Only when she felt his hot breath did she start to back away. "I know you're not going to hurt me. I know you're still in there. You have to be. Xavier wouldn't hurt me."

He lifted his upper lip, bearing his fangs, but she wouldn't show fear. She wouldn't give in. It was almost like he was trying to freak her out. She wouldn't give him the satisfaction, and not when she believed deep down every word she said.

That didn't stop her from backing up until she

hit the wooden fence bordering the garden. Nowhere to go now. He stood between her and escape, and he was so very big.

He growled louder. Goosebumps ran up and down her arms but she didn't tremble. "Xavier. I'm not afraid." She raised her right hand, only to snatch it back when he snapped at it. "Enough of that. I only wanted to see if your fur is as soft as it looks." He growled, his ears moving back and forth, eyes darting around. Was he confused?

She lowered her hand slowly, her heart in her throat, ready to pull back again if he showed her his teeth. Only he didn't. Her hand made contact with the side of his face and yes, his fur was extremely soft and thick. And he let her do it. He was breathing fast, the warmth of it hitting the inside of her wrist, but he didn't try to attack.

Suddenly, he pulled his head away and ran off into the woods. She watched, feeling hopeless and a little sad. Not for herself, but for him. Something must have happened to make him this way. Not a shifter, but one who was very afraid and unsure of himself.

"I'm surprised you were able to do that."

She whirled around to find Drake watching from the porch.

His smile was grim. "Don't worry. I fully intended to come to your rescue if things got out of hand, but you handled it well."

She let out a shaky laugh as he approached. "Are you all like this?"

"You mean skittish and temperamental? No. He's going through some unique troubles right now."

"Like what? I only want to, I don't know, try to help him. It sounds stupid now that I say it out loud. He's the one who's supposed to be helping me."

"I'm not sure there's anything you could do besides what you've already done. You tried to show him you trust him. Unfortunately, he doesn't trust himself." Drake gazed out in the direction Xavier had run.

"What is it? Why not?"

He stroked his beard. A really great beard. She wasn't normally into facial hair, but he made it work well. Her taste ran much closer toward Xavier's ever-present dark stubble. "Years ago, he was in the military. A lot of us were. And of course, when you sign up, part of your induction involves inoculations. A ton of them."

"Sure, I know that."

"In his case, they did something to him. They clashed with his wolf, I guess you could say. He's never been the same since, though he managed to hide it until recently."

Now she followed the direction of Drake's gaze. Where had he gone? How far would he run? "What does it do?"

"He can't control his shifting. When he gets good and angry, it comes over him all at once. And once he's the wolf, he can't always control what happens. That's why he doesn't trust himself around you. He's afraid he's going to hurt you without meaning to."

It suddenly seemed silly, swearing she trusted him. How was she supposed to know he couldn't control his wolf sometimes?

"Don't take it personally. If anything, it's because he wants to protect you."

"I understand."

"And until he ended up guarding you, his plan was to go off on his own. He wants to remove himself from civilization, I guess you could say. This way, he doesn't have to worry about attacking some random person."

For some reason, this struck her as just about the saddest thing she'd ever heard. "But it's not his fault."

"Of course not. But he blames himself, still. It would weigh too heavy on him, knowing he'd hurt or even killed someone else. The fact that he managed to control himself around you is remarkable, really."

She turned to him and found him wearing a strange expression. "What?"

He blinked rapidly. "What, what?"

"You had the funniest look on your face when you were staring at me just now."

"Did I? Huh. I didn't notice." He jerked his chin in the direction Xavier had fled before turning around and strolling slowly back to the house. "He'll come back. Just give him some space."

For some reason, it wasn't that easy for her. All she wanted was to run after him, to beg him to let her in. He struck her as someone who'd been alone for too long.

SHE WAS DREAMING about wolves again. This time, at least she understood why.

Her eyes opened and for a second, she didn't know where she was. Her heart raced and she went cold all over before remembering. She was safe. She was with Drake and Audra. And Xavier was right next door if she needed anything.

She hadn't seen him all day, not since he ran away. She knew he came back, though, even if she hadn't seen him. Even before she heard him in his room, in fact. It was a feeling. Something she couldn't explain. She didn't have to see him, but she knew he was there.

It would have been a comforting feeling if it wasn't for the way he kept trying to shove her out of his life. She knew she had no business being there, really, but she wanted to be. He had already done so much for her. And he needed somebody, badly. Even if he didn't think so.

The clock next to the bed read 12:45. She rolled onto her side, bunching the pillow up under her head the way she liked it before closing her eyes. Her last dream had been a doozy. She was a wolf, too, running alongside Xavier through the mountains. She never used to remember her dreams so clearly, but lately, they felt almost as real as reality. Long after she woke up she could still feel them, even smell the air.

It didn't seem too strange that she could smell the mountain air now. One of the perks of getting out of Denver—the air was cleaner, crisper somehow. One would think that would make it easier to fall into a deep sleep. Unfortunately, her brain was wide awake now. She wasn't the least bit sleepy.

And she had a craving. She and Audra had eaten ice cream on the back porch after dinner, and it had been some of the best she'd ever tasted. Butter pecan. "Probably from, like, supernatural cows or something." Audra had laughed over that, but Olivia hadn't been joking. Everything seemed just a little better in Pine Cove, a little fresh air, a little more delicious. No sooner had she licked the spoon clean than she wanted more.

Rather than wait for the morning, she got out of bed and opened the door slowly, lifting it slightly so the hinges wouldn't squeak. It was almost laughable, sneaking downstairs for a midnight snack like she was a child. As if anybody would actually care.

Somehow, the sneakiness made it a little more fun.

She crept out of the room, leaving the door ajar, before turning to head for the stairs.

And instantly walked straight into a very solid, very naked chest.

She jumped back, gasping, only to find Xavier standing in front of her. Shirtless. And with his eyes glowing in the darkness.

10

———

Of all people for him to find in the hall at this time of night.

Of all things for her to be wearing when he did.

Her nightgown was black satin, cut high up on the thigh. The straps holding it up were almost painfully thin. A tiny tug and they'd shred. His fingers twitched at the thought of it.

No, that would be a wasted effort. He could touch her just as easily through the thin satin which flowed over her luscious curves like water. For the first time in longer than he could remember, he wanted. Wanted to touch, taste, feel. To hear his name falling from her lips in the dark. His wolf perked up, not angry for once. Hungry, more like.

Her heart pounded loud enough for his heightened sense of hearing to pick it up. Her pupils dilated. Her lips parted slightly and his gaze focused there. Full, tempting. Suddenly he knew he wouldn't get a moment of sleep if he didn't learn what they tasted like.

She leaned in without saying a word until the soft satin brushed against his chest. Her pulse quickened and her scent intensified with every beat of her heart until there was nothing he could do but reach for her and pull her in until their bodies were flush, until her mouth was just within reach. She tipped her head back to invite him and he took the invitation, pressing his lips to hers the way he'd fought against doing for days.

Instead of quenching his desire, the taste of her, the feel of her in his arms turned hunger into starvation. He'd die from needing her. He'd never be able to get enough. His hands slid down her sides and over her hips, making her moan softly into his mouth. She melted against him, arms winding around his neck and pulling him down.

It would be easy to give in to what the wolf—and he—wanted next. She was willing and her arousal was obvious. She wanted him right back.

But it wouldn't be right. Not yet, anyway.

Which was why he did the opposite of what he craved most. He pulled back and already regretted the decision when he caught sight of the disappointment in her wide eyes. One of them had to be smart. "I'm sorry."

"Did I give you the impression you needed to apologize?" There was a flush on her cheeks and her already full lips were swollen thanks to the way he'd kissed her. Ripe fruit nearly bruised thanks to what she did to him and his wolf.

He pried his eyes from her chest, rising and falling fast. "Uh, what are you doing out here?"

She tried to fight back a grin. "You caught me sneaking downstairs for ice cream."

"It can be our little secret, so long as you'll let me join you. I didn't get any after dinner."

"You might not get any now if I beat you down there." She darted around him and ran full-out for the stairs before flying down them, barefoot, her hair fanning out behind her. He followed as quietly as possible. The last thing he wanted was for Drake to hear them and get in the middle of whatever was happening.

What was happening, really? He couldn't tell. But he wanted to find out.

By the time he reached the kitchen, she was

already in the freezer. "There's a whole half-gallon left. You might have to pull me away from it." She left the container on the counter before grabbing a pair of spoons from a drawer.

"Shouldn't we scoop some into bowls, or are you planning on eating straight from the carton? Don't tell me you can polish off an entire half-gallon alone."

"I'm not going to be alone, though, am I?" She flashed a grin before relenting. "Fine. No spoons directly in the container. I'll admit you're right."

"It must be my lucky night, then. You don't do that often." What was different about her now? She was lighthearted, even flirty. Was he reading the situation wrong? How could he read it otherwise? Her attitude had changed, and not the way he would've expected after what she'd seen. What he'd shown her.

She hopped up on the counter, giving him no choice but to check out her legs. "Aren't you cold?" He picked up the bowl she'd fixed and tested the ice cream, which was more than worth getting out of bed for.

She shook her head. "No, I'm fine. Aren't you?"

He looked down at himself, smirking. "I don't feel cold. We run warm."

"Good to know. I'll add that to the very short list of things I know about you." She eyed him while sliding the spoon between her lips. Yes, she was flirting. Teasing him. Especially when she licked the spoon afterward.

"Why are you doing this?" He settled across from her, leaning his back against the opposite counter. Less of a risk of reaching out and grabbing her on impulse.

"Doing what?"

"You know what." He groaned softly when she licked the spoon again. Whether she heard him or not, he couldn't say. He was making a fool of himself over her.

"I really don't know. Seems I'm eating ice cream, which I don't think I need to explain. You've tasted it. You know how good it is." She crossed her legs and he barely stifled another groan at the way the satin crept up her thigh.

"How many times do I have to try to explain it? I'm no good for you. You've seen it for yourself."

"And I wasn't afraid, remember?"

"There's a lot more to it than that."

Her smile slid away. "I know. Drake told me."

He growled, setting the bowl aside. "Drake has a

big mouth. That's not the first time he's let it run away with him."

"He saw how confused I was." She stirred what was left in the bowl, staring down at it. "And how worried I was about you."

"I'm not the one you have to worry about."

"What are you saying? I have to worry about myself?"

"Hell, yes. The way I've done ever since I set eyes on you." She flinched and he wished he hadn't said it that way. He took a deep breath before continuing. "I only meant you need to be aware of the danger I put you in. You said it yourself, Drake already told you. Why isn't that enough?"

She stirred the ice cream some more, chewing her lip. He wished he could be the one to do it. "I don't know. Because I don't feel afraid. Somehow I know you wouldn't hurt me."

"You can't know that for sure."

"I feel it."

"I, myself?" He crossed the room against his better judgment. "No. I would never hurt you while I'm the way you see me now. Thinking and acting as a man. It's when I shift that things get dangerous."

"I can handle a little danger." She wore half a

smile as she lifted her chin in defiance. "That, I'm not worried about."

Her attitude only set his teeth on edge. "Are you always like this? I thought you had sense."

"I have plenty of sense. I wouldn't have gotten as far as I have, as young as I have, without sense." Some of the light left her eyes when she said it, along with the determination in her voice. "Though who knows if I'll still have a job when this is over."

"I thought you arranged time off."

"I did." She shrugged, letting out a flat laugh. "But that's how it is sometimes. You don't know you've pushed too hard until you already have. Everybody's all smiley and encouraging to your face, but take one day longer than they think is acceptable and all of a sudden they're looking at you like you heated fish in the breakroom microwave."

"That sounds disgusting."

She stared at him. "The fish isn't the point."

"I understand what you're saying. You know, I do exist in the real world."

Her lips pursed as if she hadn't considered it. "I have a hard time remembering that. You don't seem like you're really part of the world. More like you sort of float through it."

He glanced down at himself, smirking. "I don't think I've ever floated anywhere."

"You know what I mean."

"I do. I guess you're right. We usually exist on the fringes, in a way. It's better not to mix too much with the so-called normal world."

All that made her do was snort before she set her bowl aside. "Normal. That's a joke."

"I can understand why you would feel that way."

Their eyes met, and there was a searching quality in hers that pulled him in. Not that he needed the excuse. She pulled him in without hardly trying like he was a fish on a line. He could struggle all he wanted to free himself, but it was no use. In the end, whatever unspoken thing hovered between them would win out and reel him in.

"You're the only thing right now that makes me feel even close to safe and normal." It took nothing more than the brush of her fingertips against his forearm to rouse his wolf, who perked up once again. "I'm not trying to make things harder for us. I'm really not. But you can't tell me you don't feel the same way. I sense it in you."

"You can't."

"Don't tell me what I can't do." Her hand slid up his arm, over his bicep, coming to rest on his shoulder. It was all he could do to control his baser urges. And the longer she touched him, the longer she gazed up at him with a mixture of fear and longing in her eyes, the more difficult it was to remember why he felt the need to control himself in the first place.

He had to try. She didn't understand how dangerous this was, but that was no excuse to let her lead him into what they both wanted. "What about shouldn't? Can I tell you what you shouldn't do?"

A wicked smile stirred her lips. "Only if you're okay with my doing the exact opposite."

How was he supposed to resist this? She was warm, willing, wanting him. There was nothing between them but a pitiful excuse for a nightgown that he could shred with all the effort it took to blink an eye. Didn't he deserve what he wanted? No, what he needed?

He plunged his hands into her hair, taking a moment to look deep into her eyes for any hint of reservation. All he found was the same desire currently burning him up inside.

A moment later he was kissing her again, harder than before. This wasn't a moment of mindless passion. It was a deliberate choice and the only way he knew to show her how she made him feel since he didn't have the words to express it.

She was deliberate, too, parting her legs and wrapping them around him. Pulling him in, holding him in place. Not that there was anywhere else he wanted to be. Not when she fit so perfectly against him. When her skin was the softest thing he'd ever touched. He'd never get tired of it if he touched her every day for the rest of his life.

She moved her hips, brushing up against the hardness he pressed against her, and all thoughts of her skin were replaced by other thoughts. Cravings. Everything he'd been holding back. The need to take her. Claim her for himself and his wolf. He had to make her theirs, for always. It was the way things had to be.

Olivia moaned softly into his mouth when he pressed against her and the wolf surged within him. *Take. Claim.* She was so ready and willing, arching her back like she was giving herself to him. Offering what he so desperately wanted. When he cupped one of her breasts through the satin she moaned again, and the scent of her arousal was intoxicating.

It all changed in an instant. He didn't feel it coming, too caught up in the moment. By the time he registered the shift coming over him, it was almost too late.

"What—" Olivia's breathless, half-formed question was the most she could get out as he tore himself away from her and bolted for the door. He opened it less than a moment before the shift overtook him, before blinding rage nearly drove him to do something he'd never forgive himself for.

Before the rage could get the better of him he rushed outside into the garden, away from her.

11

———

So much for timing.

She watched with a sinking heart as Xavier's wolf disappeared through the back door. The rush of cool air that flowed into the kitchen made her shiver almost violently and sent her scrambling around for something to cover herself. It would've been bad enough, caught in the cold with nothing but a nightgown and slippers on, but her skin was flushed and her body overheated thanks to what had just happened on the counter.

There were heavy jackets hanging from pegs beside the door. She darted over, arms wrapped around her trembling body, and pulled down what had to be Audra's. Drake's would have made her look like a toddler playing dress-up in her father's clothes, but Audra's jacket fit her well. Her legs were still bare, but at least half of her was warm when she stepped out onto the porch, searching the darkness.

There he was, his eyes flashing when he turned and paced the length of the garden. Back and forth, growling, making her shiver from the intensity. It was just cold enough for his breath to form clouds of vapor with every sharp exhale.

Maybe he was right. Maybe there was no point in any of this. She hated the thought of it, but what was the use of the two of them torturing themselves when nothing good would ever come of it? It wasn't enough for her to not be afraid of him. He had to feel the same way, and it was clear whatever was going on scared him half to death. Not for his sake, but for hers.

What would it be like, losing control of herself the way he did? She had no way of relating to his suffering. She was blessed with good health and had always been able to do pretty much what she wanted when she wanted to. Was it wrong to shrug off what was a very real struggle for him, all because she didn't see things the way he did?

It wasn't enough for her not to be afraid. He had to share that feeling, and he didn't. She doubted he would ever identify it as fear and she knew better than to use the word, but it was true. He was afraid. How could she help him through it?

Her feet were moving before she made the choice, taking her down the back stairs, her slippers barely making a sound on the soft ground as she approached him. Was this the craziest thing she'd ever done? If not, it had to be up at the top of the list, maybe directly beneath turning down a fortune.

He whirled around, his teeth bared as he growled. She bared her teeth right back, growling the way he did. His head snapped back a fraction and while she couldn't be sure, she thought there might be confusion in his glowing eyes.

Taking advantage of this, she reached out to touch his shoulder. He shied away, but not far enough that she couldn't reach him.

"It's okay." She patted him gently, still expecting to pull back if he snapped the way he had before. It wouldn't be his fault if he did—that didn't mean she had to serve herself up on a platter, either.

He didn't snap. He tensed, though, his breaths coming short and quick. "See? It's fine. You don't have to worry about me." He snorted and she wondered if that was a coincidence or Xavier's derision coming through. Either way, she was glad he couldn't speak just then. The last thing she felt like hearing was another argument about what was so obvious.

He continued pacing and she didn't get in his way, only reaching out to stroke his fur whenever he passed. She was half-frozen and glad no random strangers could see her standing half-naked in the garden, but nothing short of a sudden downpour would move her.

By the time his pacing slowed, his breathing had, too. No more panting, no more growling. She wanted to believe this was some sort of turning point but was afraid to get her hopes up. She settled on calling it progress.

Finally, he shifted back to his human form. The moonlight poured over his chiseled muscles. She told herself that was why she was staring openly, that she was admiring the beautiful image he created with his broad shoulders and rock-hard chest that moved with every breath. It was enough to make her own breath catch.

"See?" She ventured a smile. "You can control yourself. I knew you could."

He only scowled. "You're freezing. Let's go back inside."

There was no pretending it didn't hurt when he acted that way, so abrupt, leaving no room for discussion. But she was freezing, and pushing him any harder might only drive him away. She followed him into the house and hung up Audra's jacket before washing up the dirty bowls. Xavier offered to help, but she shook her head. "I can handle two bowls." When the tension he still carried in his shoulders eased, she knew it was the right thing to do, letting him off the hook. Giving him an out.

He headed upstairs ahead of her, then, giving her a minute to get her head on straight before going back to bed. No way would she be able to sleep after everything that had happened over the past hour, but she could at least try.

Her eyes closed and within moments she was asleep again.

And again she dreamt about wolves.

"THERE YOU ARE!" The woman behind the bar waved over her head when the four of them stepped into The Watering Hole, Pine Cove's beloved bar.

It was more than a bar, though. Even if Audra hadn't already explained it that way before the girls first visited for the inn's reopening, Olivia could've picked up on the distinction. It was a gathering place for the town, where old men played chess and regulars caught up on town gossip. Tourists visited the handful of bars and cafes scattered along Main Street, but The Watering Hole was a second home to the town's residents.

Audra waved to the bartender while Drake found them a table. The chess players were at it as always, drawing Olivia's attention as she sat down. "Do they ever do anything but play chess?"

Drake snickered. "They barely play as it is. I once saw them sit there for three hours and move their pieces maybe four or five times. They were too busy listening in on gossip while trying to make it look like they weren't paying attention."

"And arguing over football." Audra giggled fondly. "The chess board is a prop. Though Mr. Northam taught me to play. I actually got pretty good at it."

"Are you sure they didn't let you win?" Drake winked at Olivia, which earned him a playful swat from his fiancée.

"Is it my memory playing tricks on me, or did she mop the floor with you the first time you two sat down at a board?" Xavier stroked his jaw, fighting back a grin.

Drake scowled. "I said it then and I'll say it now. I hadn't played in years."

"And you didn't play then, either. She kicked your butt up and down the board before you hardly knew the game started." Xavier's laughter was rich, loud, and music to Olivia's ears. "I thank my lucky stars I was there to see it."

"You need to get out more if that's your idea of entertainment." Drake was laughing, too, and it was nice to hear. He had a kind, friendly way about him, but like Xavier, his energy could sometimes run a little intense. It wasn't always easy to relax around somebody that intense. Audra had learned how to do it, but then Audra loved him—that, and he tended to loosen up when he was with her. Like her presence soothed him somehow.

Olivia wished she could do that for Xavier. But maybe she did. Maybe that was the only reason he was able to control his rages when he was around her. Was it wrong, hoping? She was only setting herself up for heartbreak in the end. Yet she couldn't bring herself to stop wanting him.

Just then, what she wanted more than Xavier was for him to have a good time. They'd been in Pine Cove five days by then, and not once had she heard him laugh until now. "You should do more of that, you know."

He turned to her with a smile while Drake and Audra chatted with the bartender who'd stopped by with four pint glasses. "Do what?"

"Laugh. You have a nice laugh."

His eyes darted over her face, his brows drawing together in puzzlement. "You never heard me laugh before?"

"No, sir. Not until now." She lifted her glass and took a sip of the crisp lager. "You should do it more often."

"I'll make a note of that." He wore a wry smile, lifting his glass. "But don't expect me to force it."

"I wouldn't want you to." No, what she wanted was to be the reason why he smiled. Why he laughed. The way Audra was for Drake. Their happiness was so obvious, and from what Audra had shared when it was just the two of them, it seemed like Drake had gone through some rough times of his own. When he and Audra first met, he was as closed-off as Xavier. Wounded, haunted by the past.

Somehow, Audra had gotten through to him. Olivia wondered if she had the same sort of power. Maybe she could break through Xavier's reservations and convince him to take a chance on himself.

Lately, she spent more time thinking about him, wondering, wishing than she spent thinking about her very real, very dangerous situation.

It was easy to forget danger in Pine Cove, though. Bringing her there had been a stroke of genius on Xavier's part. There was no chance of anybody knowing where she was. She was sleeping better, getting plenty of exercise thanks to the help Audra needed in the garden and all over the grounds. It might've been a nice little vacation had it not been for the threats still hanging over her head. Silent or not, they were still there.

She leaned in a little, catching a whiff of his cologne. For a second it seemed like the smartest idea ever to bury her face in his neck. She managed to fight the impulse, but barely. "What about him? Is he one?" She nodded toward a man wearing a trucker hat, sitting alone at the far end of the bar. He was big, burly, and might as well have worn a sign that read *Back Off*.

In other words, he struck her as the type who'd be a shifter based on her limited knowledge of them.

Xavier scowled. "I shouldn't encourage this game."

"Who's playing a game? I only wondered."

He rolled his eyes but studied the man anyway.

"Definitely. He's from a pack northwest of Pine Cove. He once tore a man to pieces with his bare hands, then beat a second man to death with the first man's severed leg."

She gasped and clutched his arm. "No way! How can you tell that just from looking at him?"

He managed to keep a straight face for all of three seconds before laughter got the better of him. "You're way too gullible sometimes."

"You jerk." She smacked his arm the way Audra sometimes did to Drake. He didn't seem to mind. In fact, he laughed harder. This wasn't what she had in mind when she wished she could make him laugh, but it was still nice to hear.

"Not every big guy is one of us. He's a regular, run-of-the-mill human just like a handful of the people around here."

"Audra told me there's a mix of people in town."

"Yes, and they allow each other to live in peace, and they have each other's backs when need be." he looked thoughtful before taking a swig of beer, then swallowing. "Seems like there's a lesson to be learned there."

She had so many questions. What was it like having a secret like his? Was it always on his mind, the need to conceal that part of him? Would it be easier if he lived with his pack?

Was he still planning on running away?

Was she enough to keep him around?

That last question was still on her mind hours later, as they reached the inn. "It must be so nice, having somewhere like this to come home to." The stately old home almost seemed to reach out and welcome them as they pulled up in front.

"Me, I like the idea of coming home and knowing I transformed the place into something good again." He turned off the engine, gazing up at the house the way she did. "I know he's proud, and he has every right to be. Before this, he felt like he was letting his folks down, letting the place fall to pieces."

"What about your home?"

"Who says I have one?"

"You don't? Where do you live normally?"

"Around. I do have a house in Shotgun Falls, or rather outside the town, where the pack lives. But I haven't stayed there more than a few days at a time in years." He sighed, and it was just about the loneliest sound she'd ever heard. "I haven't felt like I was part of things since I got home. It's not easy to let your guard down when there's always this thing behind you. Hovering, if you know what I mean. Always, you have to guard against being found out."

"Did you ever once think the people around you would understand if you opened up and told them the truth?"

"What are you asking? Why I didn't think to give everyone around me a chance?"

"I mean, sort of? I'm not trying to be judgmental. I only want to understand."

He seemed to give it thought instead of answering right away. He made her wait just long enough that she began to regret asking in the first place. "It felt like too much of a gamble. I've never been big on gambling."

"Sure. I would probably do the same thing. That's not the kind of thing you can take back."

"Exactly." He sighed again. "Well, come on. Before they lock the doors on us." She chuckled and followed him out of the truck, then up the porch stairs. When he reached back and caught her fingers, winding his own around them, she didn't stop him. In fact, her heart soared. It was such a simple, natural gesture, and it felt like the most normal thing in the world. Why couldn't it always be this way?

"What are you thinking? A midnight snack,

maybe?" He raised an eyebrow, nodding down the hall toward the kitchen.

"No, not tonight. I already had too many fries earlier." She started for the stairs and he followed close behind. This time, her heart didn't soar. It beat frantically, fighting against her rib cage like it wanted to break loose. Neither of them had made any suggestions when it came to what happened once they got upstairs, but neither of them needed to. There was a charge in the air, almost like an electric current flowing between them. This wasn't going to end with a simple '*Sweet dreams*' before they parted ways and retreated to their rooms.

Drake and Audra were already down the hall in their suite. "Good thing I locked the front door." Xavier chuckled softly, gazing down the hall.

She bounced on the balls of her feet. Had she misread the situation? He didn't seem particularly at ease right now. "So..."

"So." He looked down at her, his mouth tipping upward at one corner. How could anyone be so handsome? Sometimes she forgot how to breathe when he looked at her. Or when she looked at him. Or when he walked into a room.

She opened her mouth, prepared to say goodnight, when he made a sound somewhere between a sigh and a growl and took her face between his hands. There was no fighting his grip. She didn't want to.

His kiss was firm, commanding, parting her lips so his tongue could dance along them. She clutched his shoulders—they were so thick and firm, and the way the muscles moved under his skin melted her into a puddle. Everything about him was enough to make her ache.

And the way he kissed her, like a man with nothing better to do and nowhere to be. Like it was all he wanted to do and for as long as possible, too. Nobody had ever kissed her the way he did.

Nobody had ever left her wanting more the way he did, either. He tried to break the kiss the way he had before, but this time she wasn't having it. "Come here." She backed into her room, still holding onto him.

"You sure about that?" He didn't exactly fight her, but he didn't go along easily, either. Still fighting with himself.

"I could use some company tonight." She pressed a kiss against his mouth, standing on tiptoe to do it, before closing the door behind him. "Simple as that."

"There's no such thing as simple when a woman drags you into her room."

She arched an eyebrow while kicking off her shoes. "You're free to go whenever you want."

He shook his head, then took off his shoes, too. "I've been called many things. Stupid has never been one of them. As long as you're not afraid I'll attack you in the middle of the night."

Afraid? She was sort of hoping he would. "I'll take my chances." She pulled him in for another kiss, playful this time, and it wasn't long before they fell into bed together.

What she needed more than she'd ever needed anything was his nearness. His warmth and strength to remind her she wasn't alone against the shadowy threats still lurking somewhere out there, haunting the edges of her dreams. Sometimes sleeping so soundly wasn't a blessing, like when it made waking up from a nightmare nearly impossible.

She had a feeling things would be different tonight, in his arms. He pulled her close, the big spoon to her little one, almost wrapping his body around hers. "You're safe with me." It was the last thing he murmured in her ear before sleep caught up to her and pulled her under. She didn't get the chance to tell him she'd known that all along.

12

It was good hunting in the hills surrounding the town. Xavier had looked forward to heading out with Drake on cold, clear mornings just after dawn, like they had during his first visit. By the time they finished their hunt a week after his arrival with Olivia, his wolf was pleasantly tired and he felt better than he had in ages.

They were roughly a half-mile from the inn when they loped down the hillside, then shifted into their human forms. The downside of interacting as their wolves was the lack of conversation, and Drake had alluded to business he needed to discuss before reaching the inn.

"You needed that. I could tell." Drake looked him up and down before nodding in approval. They took their time, moving carefully through the heavily wooded space. The land belonged to Drake, passed down for generations. He wanted to leave it wild the way it was, and Xavier could understand why. There was too much development in the world as it was. Too little space for wild animals to live the way they were intended to.

"There's never anything like a good hunt."

Drake's sly grin spoke volumes. "You've been looking a lot better as the week has gone on, too. More sure of yourself."

"Maybe I am." When Drake chuckled, Xavier bared his teeth. "Get to the point, already."

"Fine. My point—it's obvious you're falling for her, and I think she's good for you."

"I'm glad she has your approval."

"Come on." Drake shook his head. "It wasn't easy for me to come around to the fact that I found my mate, but trust me, it's a lot easier once you do. No more trying to fight off the inevitable, if you know what I mean."

"It was different for you." While he understood what his friend was trying to do, there was no shaking the sense of being misunderstood. Yes, he'd been lucky enough to control the wolf's rage the past couple of times he shifted without warning, but that was all it was. Luck. He couldn't trust luck when it came to Olivia. She was too precious already.

"Admit it, though. You're falling for her."

"Or what? You'll tell her for me? You've already done a lot of speaking on my behalf lately."

Drake winced. "Alright. I deserved that. But you know it all came from the right place."

"I do know, which is the only reason I'm still speaking to you."

"Am I supposed to be grateful for that?" Drake laughed at Xavier's growl. "Anyway, you haven't denied it, so I'll take that as affirmation."

"That's the trouble with people once they find somebody they want to settle down with. They think everybody else needs to settle down, too."

He could grumble all he wanted, but that didn't change anything. Drake was right. He'd fallen for Olivia, hard. Somewhere she'd gone from the perplexing girl whose life he was trying to protect to the perplexing girl whose life meant more than his own. How had that happened? He couldn't pinpoint a single moment. He only knew if someone came along, threatening her, he would place himself between her and the threat without thinking.

"I'm not sure if I can trust myself yet."

"I guess it's the kind of thing that can only come

with practice. Once you know you can handle it, and you don't have to give in when you feel yourself losing control, the more comfortable you'll become."

"I hope it's as easy as you make it sound."

"You've found the right woman. That much is obvious. She didn't lose it when she found out who you are. That's a pretty good sign."

"I figured she was in shock."

"She could have been in the moment. But an entire week has passed since then, and it doesn't seem like she avoids you. The opposite, actually."

"Is that how it was for you?"

"Roughly, yes. From what I understand, it was that way for Logan, too. And Nico. And Ezra."

And they were all happy, weren't they? Their mates accepted them, and they were happy. Happiness wasn't something he had ever done much thinking about. Normally, he'd been busy trying to survive. Who had time to worry about happiness?

They were closing in on the house. Drake thrust out an arm, holding Xavier back. "I wanted to talk about this before we reached the inn."

"It's about Olivia?"

Drake nodded. "I've had eyes on her apartment all week. Aside from the locksmith, there have been no further attempts at getting inside. No strange occurrences at the office, either."

"Do I even want to know how you managed to arrange all this?"

"I have my ways, which you well know." He smirked before folding his arms. "I also found out a little bit about a group who made life pretty difficult for Marcus Pemberton."

Xavier hung on his every word. "Well? Out with it."

"It was some lunatic fringe group out in California. They were trying to steal software from the company, claiming it was intended to spy on people. Now whether or not that part's true, I couldn't say. But they were determined to get their hands on it so it couldn't be released. They failed. And when they did, they turned their attention to Pemberton himself. They must have done some digging into his business practices and associates after that."

"They were blackmailing him?"

"It looks that way." Drake rubbed a hand over the back of his neck, grimacing slightly. "My contacts were able to dig up some communications between him and key members of his legal team."

"From the firm that handled his estate?"

Drake shook his head. "No, they're the lawyers

who handle the clean, legitimate side of things. I'm talking about lawyers who specialize in backdoor agreements and shady meetings in dark parking lots."

"A man with lawyers like that lives a complicated life."

"From what I understand, nobody on that side of things has taken responsibility for the explosion that killed him. Normally, at least in the underworld, word gets around. The sort of groups willing to go that far like to make sure they're getting their money's worth."

"In other words, they'd want to scare off anybody who thinks they can cross them."

"Exactly. It's a means of keeping people in line through intimidation. But there hasn't been so much as a whisper. My money is on this group."

"What would they have to gain from killing him?"

Drake stroked his beard. "It could be for the same reason an underworld boss would do it. Like we just said. Intimidation."

"Could be. Or maybe they were pissed and wanted payback for being denied."

"That's just as likely." He started off for the house,

and Xavier fell in step beside him. "Either way, it looks like the heat's off Olivia. It's been more than a week now since the press release went out. The world knows she has nothing to do with the company. They won't get any answers or information out of her."

Could it be that simple? Xavier wished it was, even more than he wished he could control his wolf the way he used to before those inoculations threw him completely out of whack.

"I know she's anxious to get back to her life." Drake glanced at Xavier, and to his credit, he at least tried to make it look like he wasn't studying his friend's reaction. "And she's worried she might lose her job."

"What are you saying? You're tired of us and want us to leave?"

Drake's laughter rang out, so loud birds took flight from nearby trees. "Are you kidding? You're free help around the place, and if Audra had her druthers, Olivia would stay here always. You're welcome to stay as long as you want."

Xavier believed him, but he knew he was right, too. They couldn't hide there forever. Olivia had a career she was proud of. She'd worked hard. If she was safe, there was no point in leaving her life behind. She had to pick up and keep moving forward. He wanted that for her.

If only he was sure she'd be safe. "I'll see how she feels about it."

"That's all you can do."

He picked up Olivia's scent on the breeze. She was already outside. His heart lightened, and something that felt a lot like happiness threatened to spread through him at the idea of seeing her. He hadn't felt this way since he was a kid with a painful, pointless crush on the prettiest girl in school. She had been enough to get him out of bed every morning, just the idea of seeing her. Sharing air with her.

Until meeting Olivia, he'd figured that sort of thing would never happen again. Meeting someone and living for the next time he'd see them.

He found her sitting on a lounge chair, covered in a blanket, a steaming mug of coffee in her hands. "Good morning. I guess I'm not the early bird, after all."

Drake laughed. "You're *an* early bird, if not *the* early bird." He shared a glance with Xavier before continuing into the house, where the sound of him and Audra chatting in the kitchen brought to mind the idea of building the same sort of life with a mate.

He found Olivia smiling up at him. "How was the hunting?"

"How do you know that's what we were doing?" There was a chair next to hers and he sat in it, though he didn't recline the way she had. He'd come off the hunt so relaxed, loose, but now the tension had stirred up again.

"Duh, Audra told me." She rolled her eyes and laughed gently. "You're so suspicious all the time."

He wasn't above laughing at himself. "It's going to take a little getting used to, opening up to a human. We spend our entire lives hiding who we are."

"I get it. I was only kidding around."

"I was talking with Drake about the intel he's gathered." Might as well get to it right away rather than leaving her hanging.

She sat up, swinging her legs over the side of the chair to face him head-on. "What did he say?"

He gave her a brief rundown, stressing the fact that there had been no further interference at her apartment. "It's up to you. If you think you'd feel safe in Denver, we can go back today. I have no problem with that."

Her bottom lip almost disappeared under her

teeth. She slid a sideways glance toward the house. "I don't know..."

"If you're unsure, that's fine. You don't have to force yourself."

"Yeah, but I have responsibilities."

"Of course." The last thing he wanted was to make her feel rushed or forced. If this were anybody else, he'd tell them exactly what needed to be done and give them a time to be packed and in the truck. If they were late, they'd have to get an Uber. Now, he would've bent over backward so long as it meant she had what she needed. Was this part of finding a mate? Drake hadn't warned him.

"What do you think?" He opened his mouth, prepared to offer a vague answer, but she cut him off. "No. Don't do that."

"Don't do what?"

"You're going to say it's my decision, and you'll support it either way."

"Damn." He shook his head mournfully, stroking his jaw. "You overestimated me."

Her face fell, eyes searching his. "What? You're going to throw me over your shoulder and carry me off to Denver? Are you seriously thinking about doing that? Because I'll chain myself to one of the radiators if—"

"Whoa, whoa." He held up his hands, laughing as hard as he dared. Any harder and she was liable to tear his head off. "Has anyone ever told you that you have a bad habit of getting ahead of yourself? You have me kidnapping you like a villain from a silent movie. Should I twist the ends of a mustache?"

"Don't laugh at me."

"Don't make assumptions." He leaned forward, one hand on her knee. "No, I wouldn't drag you back to Denver. I was kidding. I do support any decision you make. If you want to go back, we'll go whenever you think it's right. If you don't, we'll figure something else out."

Her lips twitched. "I like that."

"You like what?"

"The way you keep saying 'we'. Do you mean it? Do you want it to be the two of us?"

"If you're sure you feel safe with me." He squeezed her knee. "I promise I'll do everything I can to make sure you're safe, but I want you to be comfortable."

"That's not a problem." Her smile rivaled the sun streaming through the budding trees as she wound her fingers around his. "And you're sure you want to stay with me?"

He didn't have to think about it. "Always." When

her smile widened, he was sure his chest would crack open from the swelling of his heart.

They'd have to find a way to make this work, because he was beginning to think he couldn't live without her.

13

———

"Happy anniversary." She turned away from the counter and raised her coffee in Xavier's direction when he walked into the kitchen.

His forehead creased like he was concentrating. "Anniversary? What am I missing?"

"It's been two weeks since we moved in."

He rolled his eyes, grinning as he sidled past her to pour himself a cup. The scent of his cologne and whatever unique scent that made him who he was threatened to make her toes curl. "You know anniversary means year, right?"

"Wow, really? You'd think with all my experience as an editor, I would know what words mean." She stuck her tongue out at him, which only made him snort. "I'm just saying, it's been two weeks since we moved here."

"Since you moved here, and I became your somewhat permanent guest."

"You know what I mean." She took a sip of her drink, looking around a kitchen that still didn't feel like hers. It would take some time, she knew, but part of her was still at the old place. It would have been different if she'd made the move for some other reason, like relocating her job or deciding she wanted more space. The decision would have been made on her terms, on her time.

Instead, she'd pretty much arranged everything through a realtor while still back in Pine Cove. She had taken a tour with the very helpful, very eager broker via FaceTime. Xavier had even driven all the way back to Denver to oversee having the furniture moved to the new place. All she'd needed to do was pack her personal items, which he had helped her move as the final step.

It had all happened so fast, she hardly had time to wrap her head around it. One quick goodbye to the apartment she loved so much before riding a few miles down the road to a new, somewhat larger place nobody would know about. Well, nobody but the human resources department at work.

She hadn't even told her mother about it. Not because she wanted to keep secrets, but a lifetime of knowing the woman told Olivia the conversation would turn ugly. *If you hadn't been so stubborn and had accepted your father's money instead, you could be living anywhere in the world you wanted.* It would be the same as holding her hand over an open flame. No doubt she'd get burned.

There was sunlight in the kitchen now, thanks to a window that overlooked a beautiful park across the street. Her plants hadn't suffered too much during the week she'd been gone, and a couple of them hung in front of that window while others now lived on the deep windowsill in the living room. Her furniture worked well here, too, even though it hadn't been chosen especially for this apartment. Maybe there wasn't that much difference between one location and another. What mattered was what the renter brought to it.

She'd brought her entire life. And, evidently, a roommate. Granted, he didn't pay rent, mostly because she wouldn't let him. There was still part of her that felt like he was doing this as a favor, no matter how their relationship was developing. That was one thing they never really talked about, mostly because she was afraid to bring it up. What were they to each other? They got a little closer every day. They tended to do a lot of cuddling on the couch while watching TV. He sometimes shared her bed, though they had never done more than fool around a little before cuddling up and falling asleep.

It was sweet. That was something she'd been missing from her life without knowing it. Sweetness. Simplicity.

It was also sort of hot. There was something to be said for holding themselves back, building up to something that would no doubt be explosive once the time came. It was inevitable, she knew it, and she had a feeling he knew it, too.

But there was one thing Audra had told her when it was just the two of them, while Xavier was overseeing the moving crew miles and miles away. Once they completed the mating bond, that was it. They were joined together for life.

It was something to consider, for sure. Being joined for life. Obviously, Xavier didn't want to make any sudden moves in that direction. She appreciated that. He was thoughtful, unwilling to rush into things. She was the same way.

At least, she usually was. Not when it came to choosing new apartments, evidently, but this was a different sort of situation.

"What did you have in mind for today?" She spread jelly over a piece of toast and took a big bite on her way to the refrigerator, where her lunch waited.

"I wanted to paint the bathroom today." They had gone out and chosen colors for the different rooms, with Xavier offering to do the work since he didn't have a job to head off to. What would that be like, not having to work? From the way he explained it, the pack's original founders had set it up so nobody would ever want for money. The wealth they founded had trickled down through generations, growing thanks to shrewd investments. Sure, if they wanted to work, they could. They just didn't have to. That, on top of his pension from the military, meant he was set.

"I can't wait to see it." She polished off her meager breakfast before kissing his cheek in passing. "Maybe we should go out and get something to eat after work?"

"That sounds good." The fact that he didn't hesitate gave her hope. He was finally relaxing. He didn't immediately balk at the idea of being around big groups of people.

Not that his wolf hadn't gotten away from him once or twice in the past couple of weeks, unfortunately. But it had always happened when they were alone together, and she had managed to talk him through it. It hadn't taken long for him to regain control, either. It was enough to give her hope that he would regain complete control in time.

Since it was supposed to be a beautiful night, they decided to choose a restaurant where they could eat outdoors. Somewhere he could make a quick exit if he needed to. She promised to do a little research on her lunch break before they headed out so he could drop her at the office before he made a stop at the hardware store for a few more supplies.

It was almost scary in a way, how easy it was to fall into this comfortable routine. He dropped her off at work and picked her up at the end of the day. They had dinner together, watched a movie or a show. Sometimes they would only read, with music playing low in the background. It was enough simply to spend time together, to know he was there with her.

And he seemed content, too. The restlessness she'd sensed when he first stayed with her had dissolved, probably because his confidence was growing. He didn't have to constantly question himself. And since weeks had passed since the last threat on her life with no sign of further trouble, he had less to keep an eye out for.

"Good morning." Lauren had developed a habit of sounding suggestive when she greeted Olivia first thing. This morning was no exception. "And how was your night?"

"I swear to God, we need to find you a boyfriend."

"I have a boyfriend."

"Then the two of you need to spice things up so you'll stop obsessing over what is or isn't happening in my bedroom." Olivia dropped her things on her desk, shaking her head. "And for what it's worth, it's not happening."

"Why not? He's living with you, for God's sake. Is there something here you're not telling me?"

You have no idea. It took every ounce of her self-control to keep from laughing or giving herself away somehow. "We're just, you know, roommates right now. And it helps me sleep better at night."

"But nothing's happened in weeks. No threats, no burglaries. Don't tell me he's still staying with you for protection."

"What if he is? What would be so weird about that?"

"This is me you're talking to."

"It's complicated. Let's just leave it at that, okay? But things are great. Really."

"If you say so..." Lauren left a thick manuscript on her desk. "These revisions came in overnight, so I printed them out for you." Olivia blew out a heavy sigh when she spied the enormous stack of paper she now had to read through. It would've been simpler to do everything on the computer, but some of the publisher's longstanding authors didn't like doing things that way. They preferred to see everything laid out in front of them in red ink. Thankfully, this was the second round of revisions and there wasn't much that needed to be done besides a little clean-up work.

It was one of those days. No sooner did she sink into her zone of concentration than her phone rang or her inbox pinged with a new message. There were two last-minute meetings placed on her calendar before lunch, and another in the middle of the afternoon. Funny. She had always loved days like this before. The fast pace, the sense of never knowing what to expect.

That was before she had somebody at home, painting the bathroom a pretty shade of deep sapphire blue she had fallen in love with the second they saw samples at the hardware store.

That was before she had something else to look forward to.

By four o'clock, it was obvious she wouldn't be leaving anytime soon. She pulled out her phone to send Xavier a text, figuring he'd be too busy to answer a call right away. *I'm going to be held up for a while. Would you mind if we picked up something on the way home, instead? I'm not sure when that will be, but I need to get through a mountain of paper before I get out of here.* She took a picture of the current state of her desk before sending the message off to him.

He didn't leave her waiting for long. *No problem. Though I'm anxious for you to get home and see how things look. I think you'll like it. Let me know when you're ready for pick up.* She smiled to herself, biting her lip. Wouldn't it be nice if this was how things could always be? Later on, they would sit down for dinner and talk about their days. They might do the dishes together. And later tonight, she would fall asleep in his arms—if she wanted to, which she very much did. He never assumed he was welcome in her bed. Just another thing to love about him.

In fact, she loved just about everything about him. She was starting to suspect she might love him. Somehow, that felt just as right as everything else.

She was so busy reading and keeping track of the

changes she'd suggested that she hardly noticed the rest of the office heading out. She'd offered a distracted goodbye to Lauren and to a few others who had passed her open door, but otherwise, she'd been too absorbed to pay much attention. When she checked the time and found it was already 7:30, she had to rub her eyes and do a double-take. Xavier might be worried if she left him hanging much longer. She only had a few chapters left to go and decided to leave them until morning, since her growling stomach wouldn't be ignored much longer.

At the sound of footsteps, she smiled. "You know, I was just about to text you." She got up and went to the door, poking her head out to greet Xavier as he approached.

Only it wasn't Xavier. It took a second for her brain to catch up to what her eyes were telling her. Worlds collided in her head. "Mom?" She took a few steps out into the hall, her pulse picking up speed. "What happened? What are you doing here?"

The word to describe her was *disheveled*. Something her mother rarely was. Her hair was mussed, her clothes rumpled. Almost like she'd been roughed up a little bit. "What happened to you?"

It was the wild look in her mother's eyes that stopped Olivia before she could rush over to her.

Something was very wrong. "We need to talk about your father's money."

Olivia froze. "What? What are you talking about? Why did you come here?"

"I came here to talk about your father's estate." She was shaking. That was one of the many random things Olivia's increasingly panicked brain picked up on. The way she shook and the wild look in her eyes.

"I already told you, Mom. That's done. I signed everything over to the board. I didn't want any of it. Why is that not enough for you?" And why would she come all this way over something that was already a done deal? Was she this delusional?

More footsteps. Olivia's stomach dropped at the sight of three men rounding the corner from the reception area.

Though it wasn't the men themselves that chilled her blood. It was the guns they carried.

"You're sure you signed everything over?" One of the men snarled at her, menacing, before taking her mother by the arm. "Because that's not what we want to hear."

She wasn't about to show them how terrified she was, lifting her chin instead of cowering. "What is this? Get the hell out of here, all of you. You don't belong here."

"Your mom was right about you. You're a stubborn little thing." They advanced on her, giving her no choice but to back into her office. She was too panicked to close the door—not that it would have mattered. She had no doubt they would've broken in no matter what she tried to do.

"I asked you what this is all about." She still sounded hard, cold, but there was now a tremor in her voice. She could only pretend to be strong for so long.

"What does it look like?" The man holding her mother shoved her into the room. "We're going to have a little talk, and you're going to do exactly what we say."

"Please, Olivia. Do what they say." Her mother shook, her eyes wild, her voice nothing more than a hoarse whisper. "Please. Just do what they say."

"I can't do whatever it is you want. I don't have power here. I already—"

"Shut up." One of the men, thin and wiry compared to the tall, burly man shoving her mother around, pushed her into her chair before pulling out a length of nylon rope from inside his jacket.

"What are you planning to do?" And how long could she stall until Xavier showed up? He had to. Eventually, he'd sense something was wrong. He had to be wondering by now why she hadn't called or texted. If only she had thought to text a few seconds earlier.

The man gripping her mother's arm gave her a nasty smile. "What we've been trying to do all along. We're going to get what we want. And you're going to get it for us."

14

———

Xavier glanced up at Olivia's office building after crossing the final intersection on the way to picking her up. She hadn't called, but it was past 7:30. There was working late, and there was this.

He admired her work ethic, but there was a time when she had to think about herself. By now, she had to be starving. Was this the way she used to work before they met? And there he was, thinking he'd lived a solitary existence.

The parking lot was almost empty when he pulled in. She probably wouldn't appreciate him showing up unannounced, but she would have to deal with it. It was his protective nature. Just because there was no further threat from whatever group had killed her father, that didn't mean he'd stop worrying about her.

Strange. He actually enjoyed having someone to worry about, somebody to care for. She gave him something to do beyond thinking about himself and obsessing over his out-of-control wolf. He wasn't so out of control anymore—there were still moments of doubt, but they'd become fewer and farther between. He knew better than to completely attribute this to her, but facts were facts. She could talk him down, could get through to the wolf. That had to mean something.

The lobby was empty. The absence of a security guard struck him as strange, but then maybe the guy was taking a break. At this time of night, Xavier doubted many people came in. Judging by the number of cars in the lot, there couldn't be more than a small handful of people in the entire building. He took the elevator up to her floor, imagining her surprise at him showing up unannounced. Somebody had to save her from herself when she got so caught up in her work that she lost track of time.

The elevator doors opened, and he turned toward the empty reception area.

Instantly, he smelled fear on the air. Then he picked up another scent. Strangers.

His shifter hearing allowed him an idea of what was going on without the need to move closer. There were voices coming from down the hall, in the direction of Olivia's office. Deep voices, for the most part. Occasionally they were punctured with a woman's voice, a woman who wasn't Olivia.

"Just give them what they want." The woman, whoever she was, whimpered. "This can all be over if you just give them what they're asking for. For your own sake, if not mine."

"I'm telling you, it's out of my hands." Olivia. There was no pain in her voice, though that gave his wolf no comfort. She was still in danger.

"Sweetheart, nobody believes that." Sweetheart. Her mother? What did she have to do with this?

He crept closer to her office, his back to the wall. Her door was open. He inched closer, closer, until he caught sight of her.

The wolf threatened to burst through once she came into view. Her wrists were tied to the arms of her chair. There were three men in total, all of them brandishing guns. Fury filled him, his blood boiling, his head pounding. Did it really take three men to subdue one woman?

No, two women, only the one he identified as Olivia's mother wasn't tied up. She sat in a chair, though, with one of the men standing behind her. He kept his gun trained at her temple.

Olivia's eyes went wide. She couldn't see him from this angle, and he doubted she would notice him even if she could. All of her attention was focused on her mother. "Mom, call them yourself. Call the lawyers. They'll tell you. I have no right to any of it now that I signed it away."

"Undo it. It can't be that difficult." The man standing behind the older woman jammed the gun against her head harder than before. Olivia winced at the sound of her mother's whimper. "Make a phone call."

"I don't understand why you're doing this. What does any of this have to do with any of you? Who are you?"

"That doesn't concern you." One of the other two men raised his arm as if he was prepared to hit her. Xavier growled softly but held himself in place. He didn't want to give himself away this soon, not with three guns in the room.

Olivia. So brave, so fierce. She didn't so much as flinch or even blink, glaring up at the man threatening her. "What, does it make you feel good? Do you feel like a man when you hit a woman who's tied up?"

Her mother made a choking sound. "Olivia, don't do that. You don't know what these men are capable of."

"I have a pretty good idea." To everyone's surprise, including Xavier's, she spat on the floor. "That's what I think about you, you murderers. And for what? Some money? You're pathetic."

The third man, who up until this point had stood slightly apart from the rest, shook his head when it looked like his partner was about to make good on his threat. "Don't let her bait you. We need her able to speak clearly when she makes the phone call."

Olivia blew out a frustrated sigh. "What phone call? Are you all completely deluded? I can't help you."

"Sweetie, you have to try. You at least have to try." Her mother was on the verge of tears. They must have taken her against her will and brought her all this way as an added threat. What wouldn't they stop at?

He had seen more than enough. He backed slowly away, coming to a stop around the corner from the room. He would have to get two of them out of the way before going in. Only then would he like his odds.

He looked around for something to use as a distraction to draw them out. There was a cubicle close by filled with pictures. He recognized Olivia's assistant in more than one of them. He doubted she would mind a little damage if it meant helping her friend.

Which was why he picked up a snow globe, testing the weight in his hand before tipping over her empty chair. It crashed to the floor louder than he'd expected. He crouched behind the half wall, waiting to strike.

"What was that? Is there somebody else here?"

"I didn't think there was." Now there was fear in Olivia's voice. Did she know he was there? Was she afraid one of her friends was about to get dragged into this?

"Go see what that was all about."

Xavier held his breath, willing himself to wait until the right moment. Everything in him was screaming to attack, to kill, but the odds still weren't in Olivia's favor.

Footsteps rang out on the other side of the wall an instant before one of the men rounded the opening and stepped into the cubicle, staring down at the chair.

Xavier was swift, springing up from a crouch and bringing the snow globe down on the man's skull. He let out a choked groan before his body sagged. Xavier caught him before he could collapse, silencing what might have been a telltale crash against the floor. He set the man down in a corner, out of sight.

A voice rang out from inside the office. "Well? What did you find?" Xavier waited, ears tuned to any sound coming from inside the room. The men muttered to each other, but Olivia was silent. What was she thinking? What was she feeling?

"Damn it, Bill, this isn't the time to screw around." Xavier barely had time to hide before loud, strident footsteps cut through the air. The second man stepped into the cubicle, saw his friend slumped in the corner, but had no time to react before Xavier knocked him out, too. This time he took no pains to conceal him, only disarming both men before approaching the office on silent feet.

"We're not leaving this place until you make the phone call." From the sound of it, this was the one who until this point had stood off to the side. He was the leader, Xavier surmised. He didn't want to get his hands dirty, but very much enjoyed telling others what to do. And he was armed. Xavier couldn't allow himself to forget that.

"I don't even know who you want me to call. What do you want from me?"

"Don't you know?" Xavier turned the corner, revealing himself in the doorway. "They want the software they tried to blackmail your father into giving them."

Olivia gasped. So did her mother. The armed man didn't, whirling on him with the gun aimed at his chest. "What are you doing here? Who are you?"

Xavier only had eyes for Olivia, who was staring at him. Her heart was racing hard enough, loud enough for him to hear several feet away. "Are you alright?"

"I'm fine." Her eyes darted to the armed man before returning to his. "But I'd be better if the wolf was here."

The man snorted, looking around. "The wolf? What is this all about?"

Xavier ignored the question when he noticed Olivia's hands moving on the arms of the chair. She had loosened her restraints enough to free herself. Her eyes then cut to her mother, and he got the message. But was it a good idea?

As it turned out, the choice wasn't his to make. Not when the man holding the gun pressed his hand, charging forward like he was ready to attack.

"Mom!" Olivia bolted from the chair and threw herself over her mother, knocking them both to the floor.

That was when he did it. When he allowed the wolf to have its way, taking control. The exhilaration of letting go was like none he'd ever felt before. Within moments, the shift was complete, and the armed man was left gasping in surprise. His face went gray as he stumbled back, bouncing off Olivia's desk. "What the—"

Xavier gave him no time to finish the question, lunging for him. The man fought and kicked, screaming, reaching for Xavier's eyes like he wanted to gouge them out. Never a good idea to place one's hands so close to the mouth of a wolf. Xavier sank his fangs deep into the man's flesh and relished his scream of agony.

Yes. Yes, this, this was what he needed. To destroy. To drink his blood, to bathe in it. He released the hand, now mangled and almost unrecognizable, in favor of tearing at the man's throat. Screams quickly turned to gurgles, which then turned to silence. Xavier lifted his head to meet the man's sightless eyes, the flow of blood slowing until it was little more than a trickle as the heart stopped beating.

A gunshot rang through the air.

He whirled around, stunned, searching for the source of the sound. Olivia was slow in getting to her feet—and when she turned toward him, her hands were clasped over a bloodstain that began to spread over the front of her blouse.

In his shock, he shifted to his human form, and then moments later understood everything once he looked to the other woman.

"What have you done?" Olivia's mother sat up, still brandishing the pistol she'd used to shoot her daughter. "You've ruined everything! This was supposed to be simple! You couldn't do what I needed you to do just this once!"

"Mom?" That was all Olivia managed to whisper, leaning against her desk.

Her mother raised the gun as if to take another shot. That was enough to stir him out of his shock, to send him lunging for her. It took almost no effort to disarm her, then to use the gun against her head. She sank to the floor, a trickle of blood leaking from her scalp.

"Olivia, no." He caught her before she could hit

the floor. So much blood. Too much. "Stay with me. Keep your eyes open. Stay awake."

Her eyes were open, darting around, her breathing more labored with every inhale. "I tried. I didn't know..."

"Of course you didn't." With her head in his lap, he reached for the phone on her desk and punched in the number for the police. He rattled off the building's address and the location of the office and begged for help in a voice he hardly recognized as his own.

He then let the receiver fall to the floor in favor of cradling Olivia. "We need to get pressure on this." He took off his jacket and pressed it against her abdomen as hard as he dared. She winced, grinding her teeth. "I'm sorry. I'm sorry, I know it hurts. You're going to be fine."

She reached up, her fingers grazing his jaw. "Thank you for coming to get me."

Yes, but what good had it done? She was dying, he felt her dying. He heard her heartbeat growing fainter. "Please, stay with me. Don't go. Don't leave me. You can't leave me now." The wolf howled in his head, mournful, helpless. They were both helpless.

They had both allowed this to happen. They had

dropped their guard, never imagining a mother would have it in her to shoot her own daughter.

He lowered his head, pressing his lips to her forehead. She was already too cold. He held her closer, trying to warm her. "Hang on. Please hang on. You're stronger than this. Don't you dare give up."

"Hurts..." Her eyes slid shut, but he shook her until she opened them again. "My mom... hurts..." Her chin quivered.

"I know, baby. I know." He kissed her forehead again. "You can rest once the paramedics get here and they start taking care of you. But not until then." The bleeding wouldn't stop. No matter how he tried, he couldn't make it stop. What was the point of finding her if he was going to lose her this way?

"Hurts so much..." Her voice was weaker all the time.

"Don't try to talk. Save your strength." Her eyes closed again. "Olivia. Open your eyes. Look at me. Stay with me."

This time, she didn't obey. This time, her head lolled against his shoulder, the beating of her heart almost too faint to hear. He rocked her back and forth, whispering her name, kissing her, until the paramedics came charging down the hall to take over.

15

E verything hurt.

Olivia groaned softly, then winced in greater pain when she tried to move. There was a fire in her belly. White-hot, excruciating fire. Like somebody had jammed a lump of burning coal in her stomach and sewed it shut.

There was a beeping sound, high-pitched, whining. It had the effect of an icepick in her ears. She opened her mouth, prepared to ask somebody to shut the damn thing off, but she couldn't catch her breath. Her throat was so dry, her lips chapped. She tried to swallow but even that was difficult. Why was she so weak?

"Can you hear me?"

The sound managed to work its way through the

haze of pain and confusion. It was enough to calm her down. Xavier. Xavier was here. He would tell her what happened, why she was in so much pain. And why there was a sense of something tapping at the back of her mind, something that wouldn't let her go. What was it? What was she forgetting? It had to be important since it wouldn't leave her alone. But what was it?

"I'm sorry. I'm so sorry."

What was he sorry for? Her eyelids fluttered—even they were so heavy, a million pounds each. She forced them open long enough to catch sight of him sitting next to her bed. She recognized it as a hospital bed. She was in the hospital. Right. Because...

"I had to stay long enough to be sure you would make it." He took her hand, pressing the back of it to his stubbled cheek. "I couldn't go without knowing you survived."

Go? Her eyes threatened to close again but she struggled against that, and against her dry mouth and the weakness that made it so hard to catch her breath. She had to stop him. She had to beg him not to leave. Why would he go now? Why wouldn't he give her the chance to make him stay with her?

He grazed her knuckles with his lips, his eyes

closing. "You will always be with me. This is the hardest thing I've ever had to do."

Then don't do it! The beeping sound got faster, and somewhere in her half-conscious state, she understood it was her blood pressure rising. He was leaving her.

She managed to whisper a single word. "Don't." It was enough to wipe her out. She had no choice but to sink back into darkness, where there was no pain and no sense of helplessness.

The next time she woke up, the sunlight that had been streaming through the window was replaced by darkness. She opened her eyes more easily this time, and they stayed open. She looked around the room, noting the flowers and balloons lined up on the counter across from the foot of the bed.

"She's awake." The voice came from her right, and Olivia turned her head to find Megan beaming, her eyes filled with tears. "Thank God." Nico stepped up behind Megan, rubbing her back as he smiled down at Olivia.

"What happened?" She searched the room, her heart clenching. "Where's Xavier?"

"Here. Drink some of this. It will help you feel a little better." Megan held a foam cup to her mouth, a straw poking out of the top. "It's only water. I'm sure you could use it. Just take your time with it." Olivia took a few sips, sure she had never tasted anything so heavenly as plain ice water.

The next time she tried to speak, it was easier. "What happened?"

"You can't remember?" Nico sighed. "It's probably just as well."

"It's all fuzzy. I was at the office. And then..." She squeezed Megan's hand tight when it all came flooding back. "My mom. Where is she? Why did she do it?"

"I'm so sorry, honey." With her free hand, Megan stroked Olivia's hair. Tears rolled down her cheeks, but she made no attempt to stop them. "I'm so sorry that happened to you."

"I was trying to protect her. That was why I threw myself on top of her. But then she..." She couldn't bring herself to say it. She could barely bring herself to think it. Even now, lying in a hospital bed as evidence, she didn't want to believe it. Her own mother had shot her.

Nico cleared his throat, looking distinctly uncomfortable. "You might want to wait until you're feeling a little stronger before you hear all of this."

"No. No way. I'm not going to be able to rest until I know why she did it."

"I told you." Megan grinned up at him before turning to Olivia.

He shrugged. "Well, first things first. She had been seeing a man for the past six months or so."

"For that long? I didn't even know she had a boyfriend."

"He might have wanted to keep it that way."

Megan interjected. "And let's be honest, you two weren't exactly close in the first place."

"That's true. What's he got to do with this?"

"For starters, he was found dead on your office floor."

She gasped, then instantly regretted it. The pain wasn't as sharp or intense as it had been when she first woke up, and she assumed they'd given her medication for it, but the sudden intake of breath hadn't done her any favors. Once the pain passed, she was able to speak. "He was one of them?"

"It seems like whatever you witnessed was a ruse. A way of convincing you to do what they wanted. if you thought she was in danger, you would be more likely to play along."

"So she wanted the money? That's what I don't understand."

Megan gave her a sympathetic frown. "Honey. Those men who came to your office were the same ones who killed your father and tried to kill you. They were the ones who blackmailed him for that software. It turns out one of them used to work for your father. He was one of the original developers."

"And once employee records were opened after he spilled his guts to the cops, it all came together." Nico drew up a chair beside Megan's and settled in. "He was fired seven months ago for attempting to sell the technology to a competitor. That competitor was the man who later became involved with your mother. Now, that could've all been part of his ultimate plan. Once he knew he couldn't get the technology, he pulled this disgruntled ex-employee into his orbit before ingratiating himself with your mother." He shook his head, growling. "I have to give him credit for sticking to his long game the way he did. He spent half a year dating her. I doubt it was a coincidence."

"Probably not." Olivia closed her eyes, letting out a slow breath. "Damn it, Mom."

"He spent these six months convincing her your father's company had no right to use that technology for themselves, twisting everything around to make it look like the fired employee was the victim. That his ideas were stolen, and he was discarded. Like it was all an attempt to discredit him."

"I doubt he would have needed to try that hard." Olivia giggled. "When it comes to men, my mother tends to be blind to everything she doesn't want to see. He was a good-looking man. I'm sure she fell for him easy." Yes, and now he was dead, the way he deserved to be.

"Obviously, you know their attempted blackmail of your father went nowhere. Your mother confessed to the police that she tried to use your father's past connections against him, but he still wouldn't budge. He was in the right here. He had every reason to stand up to them. They had no right to the software."

"But that wasn't good enough."

"Unfortunately not. According to your mother, it was her boyfriend's idea to kill your father once she told him you were his sole heir."

"I didn't even know she knew." Then again, it seemed like she'd managed to keep a lot of secrets.

Megan sighed. "She never guessed you would turn it down."

"She never did know me very well." She turned her face away from them, looking out the window. There was nothing to see, only dark sky, but she knew if she looked at Megan just then she would start sobbing. It would hurt too much to do that. "So

I guess that means she knew what they did to me. She had to, right?"

"She hasn't been as open with that. Her story keeps changing."

"How do you know all this?"

"Drake has a friend in the police department. He sort of hooked us up so I could get information from him."

Something occurred to her. Her head snapped around. "What about what Xavier did? How are they going to explain that away?"

"That's the beauty part of having a friend on the police force. There's nothing to worry about."

"But he killed that man."

"Yes, that armed man who we now know tried more than once to kill you. From what I'm hearing, he wasn't exactly careful about covering his tracks. He may as well have been writing a manual on how to bumble his way through crime. In situations like that, law enforcement isn't exactly going to bend over backward to find out how they died. If anything, I'm sure they figure Xavier did them a favor by getting him out of the way. His accomplices have come to, and they've corroborated everything your mother has already confessed."

Her mother. Her own mother tried to kill her.

And all for money. "I guess they figured they'd make a ton if they sold the software themselves."

"No doubt."

"I can't believe I came from her. How could she be that cold? I mean, we were never really close, but I thought she at least loved me."

"I'm sure she did—and does." Megan patted her hand. "But she was in too deep. They had already gone so far. I guess at that point it was almost like an obsession. They couldn't give up after they'd already worked so hard to get their hands on the software."

Olivia sneered, bitter. "Worked hard? The woman never worked hard a day in her life. The most effort she's ever put into anything was when she pulled the trigger."

The door opened, and it couldn't have happened at a better time. She was starting to make her friends uncomfortable. A pretty, cheerful nurse in colorful scrubs stepped into the room. "You're awake. Good. How are you feeling?"

"Like I got shot in the stomach." She tried to smile but knew it couldn't look much better than a grimace.

"You'll find she's always this charming and pleasant." Megan winked at her, smiling fondly.

"Nobody is charming and pleasant when they've

been hurt like this." The nurse was gentle with her, asking questions about pain levels, taking her temperature and other vital signs before lifting her gown to look at the stitches. Nico turned away, a gesture that Olivia found touching, but Megan watched. Her stricken expression told Olivia everything she needed to know. She didn't want to see the damage for herself. Feeling it was enough.

"Your stitches are looking good. We're going to want to keep a close eye on them to make sure there's no infection. But your temperature is completely normal, so that's a good sign." The nurse pulled out a couple of syringes and explained what they held. "I'm going to flush your line with a little saline, then give you something for the pain. How does that sound?"

"That sounds amazing."

"It will make you sleepy, though." She looked to Megan and Nico. "Of course, visiting hours ended around half an hour ago."

"No way were we leaving until you woke up again." Megan squeezed her hand.

"You should go, though. You already came all this way."

"What, did you think we would actually go all the way back to the cabin? No way, girl. We're staying in town until you're ready to go home." Olivia opened her mouth to protest, but Megan only shook her head. "I've been on the group chat all day. Everybody has already arranged to take a little time off in shifts so we can take care of you at home. You're going to need a little help getting around so you don't end up tearing your stitches or, you know, hurting yourself somehow."

"It shouldn't take more than a couple of weeks." The nurse finished with the medication, and sure enough, a feeling of delicious warmth started to spread through Olivia's body.

But one more question needed to be answered before she could allow herself to give in to the promise of pain-free sleep. "Where is Xavier? He should be the one helping me. He's been staying with me. Why won't he be there?"

Megan looked at Nico, who looked very much like he wished he was anywhere but there. "Xavier decided to go. Like he was originally planning to do."

"You're not serious." Now she remembered him sitting at her bedside, saying goodbye. Why hadn't she tried harder to stop him? "Where did he go?"

"He wouldn't say." He was obviously angry but holding back for the nurse's sake.

Megan rubbed her arm. "Honey, you shouldn't get upset right now."

"Screw that." She glared at Nico. "How could you let him go?"

"With all due respect, it wasn't up to me to make him stay. He'd made up his mind. I told him how unhappy it would make you, but he was determined."

Damn her heavy eyelids. They wanted to close, to block out everything, and part of her wanted that very much. She didn't want to think about life without him. The home they were starting to build together. How could he leave like that?

How could he leave her? He never even gave her a chance to ask him to stay, but that was probably a deliberate choice. He didn't want to have to face her. Did that make him a coward? She wouldn't have used the word to describe him before now, not by a long shot. It turned out there was more than one way to be cowardly. He could throw himself at an armed man but he couldn't stand saying goodbye while she was conscious.

"Just get some sleep now, okay?" Megan stood, leaning over to kiss her forehead. "We'll come around to see you tomorrow. Charlotte and Hope are coming out and we're going to stay at your place if you don't mind."

"I don't mind." Olivia's eyes closed—she didn't have the strength to stay awake anymore, and her heart hurt too much. "You'll have to let me know what you think about the new paint."

16

There was nothing like a long hike to clear his head. The days were growing longer and warmer all the time, giving him the opportunity to head out for longer periods. To enjoy the fresh air, the sense of being part of the wilderness. This was where his kind belonged. Not in cities, crammed in with so many other people. They needed space, room to roam.

So what if it meant being alone?

He was getting used to that. In time, he might grow to enjoy it. Once he forgot everything else he'd been on the verge of enjoying. Companionship. Partnership. The love of his mate.

Plenty of wolves lived without mates. He'd be one of them.

Because he didn't deserve her. Every single day since the shooting, he'd replayed the events in his head. It was his own private movie, running on a loop. The mistakes he'd made. He hadn't so much as suspected Olivia's mother carried a gun. He'd made the assumption she was an injured party, that she'd been forced into going to Denver to convince her daughter to save them both.

And Olivia had almost paid with her life. How could he ever forgive himself? How could he ask her to forgive him or love him after that? No, it was better this way. Alone, in the mountains a few hours north of Denver. For now, he was comfortable at the cabin he'd rented. Only Nico knew where it was located, and that was more a matter of acquiescing to his friend's demands when he knew he'd never hear the end of it otherwise.

By the time the cabin came into view, he'd been out for hours and the sun was beginning to sink. The sight of the weathered, pine walls and shingled roof brought him a sense of peace. He told himself that would have to be enough. That he needed to forget the work he'd been putting into the apartment he'd almost fled from. The sense of pride in building a home with the woman he loved.

The woman he loved. He had never told her. It

was probably better that way. Easier for her to move on. She deserved that, no matter how badly the idea of her being with another man tore at him.

When a familiar scent reached his nose, he told himself it was a trick his wounded heart was playing on him. That had to be it. Otherwise, it would mean Olivia was there. That the scent of her skin and soap and shampoo and the detergent she used on her clothes, now flowing his way on the easterly breeze, was due to her presence. That couldn't be. Nico had sworn he'd keep the location of the cabin to himself.

Stupid of him, assuming that promise would be kept.

He rounded the cabin, still a few hundred yards out, and there she was. Standing on the porch, arms folded, looking around like she was searching for any sign of him. How long had she been there? How long would she wait if he never arrived, if he simply kept walking into the mountains?

The fact was, he didn't want that. He didn't want to keep her waiting. He didn't want to hurt her anymore, the way he knew he must have.

And he didn't want to hurt without her. The sight of her brought to mind raindrops falling on parched earth. He had only thought he understood how much he missed her. Seeing her now, it was all so raw, so overwhelming, it was almost enough to knock him off his feet.

Did she hear him? Did she sense him somehow? Her head snapped around, eyes seeking him. They found him and almost pierced him, her gaze was so intense even at a distance. He raised a hand in greeting before continuing, closing in on the cabin. She waited until he was only a few dozen feet away before drawing a breath so deep her chest puffed up. He was in for it. He was too glad to care.

"What did you think you were doing, leaving me like that?" She stomped down the plank stairs before marching to him. Her arms swung almost violently at her sides, hands tightened into fists. "You didn't even give me a chance to tell you how much I wanted you to stay. You took away my chance to say goodbye. What was that supposed to be? What am I supposed to think?"

He waited until she stopped to take a breath. "Hi."

"Don't try to be cute right now. I'm not in the goddamn mood for you to be cute. If I thought it would make the slightest difference, I'd hit you. But you wouldn't feel it." She tossed her hair over one shoulder, glaring at him with the intensity of a hurricane. The comparison fit. She'd had the effect of a hurricane, tearing up his life and the way he saw himself.

"Would it make a difference if I told you how hard it was for me to leave?"

"No. What, am I supposed to feel sorry for you? You know what was hard? Healing up from getting shot in the stomach and not even having you with me. That was hard." Her voice cracked, revealing the depth of pain behind her attack. That was Olivia in a nutshell. She was all flash and fire on the outside, but inside there was an enormous and easily wounded heart.

"You weren't alone, though, were you? Megan was already talking about getting your friends together to help out."

"It wasn't the same. I love them, but it was you I wanted. You understood everything that went on. You knew how I felt and what I was going through. It was you I needed."

"It seemed like the right thing to do at the time, even though I didn't want to go."

"So why did you?"

"Didn't Nico tell you?"

"Forget Nico." She jabbed a finger against his chest—and she was right, he barely felt it. "I want to hear it from you. Why did you leave?"

Now, looking back, it all seemed useless. Childish, even. At the time, however, he'd been sure he was making the right decision. "It was my fault you were shot."

"It was my mother's fault because she was the one who pulled the trigger. That had nothing to do with you."

"I shouldn't have let my guard down. I was too busy focusing on killing that guy, I forgot about her."

"You didn't know she was a threat."

"I shouldn't have given her the opportunity. I didn't protect you."

She threw her hands into the air. "I didn't expect it, either. I didn't think you had to protect me anymore. You did exactly what I knew you'd do. You ended that guy. You saved me. Neither of us could've predicted what she'd do."

He reached for her, taking her arms in his hands. "How are you doing with that? I've wanted so much to ask. You have no idea how many times I almost called."

"Almost. But you still didn't." She sighed, her shoulders slumping. "I'm getting through it. That's the best I can say."

"And how are you feeling?"

"I'm doing well. I took some time off from work

to heal up. I'm not sure I can go back there, at least not to the office."

"I can't imagine that would be easy for anybody." He rubbed her arms, so grateful she didn't try to stop him. "Would you believe it if I told you I missed you?"

"Honestly? I'm not sure. If you miss somebody, how do you not reach out to them? Or respond to messages? Didn't you ever wonder if I was okay?"

"Are you kidding? I had Nico checking in with me every hour until you were out of the hospital, and then he'd feed me any information he got from Megan after that."

"So he knew where you were all along."

"Eventually. But he always knew how to reach me. I couldn't go without knowing how you were holding up. I don't want you to think I forgot you. I could never forget you."

"But you left me." Her chin trembled. "And I missed you. And I needed you."

"And I was the biggest idiot who ever lived for leaving. I see that now." He did, too. He saw how pointless it was, removing himself from her life. It was his pride getting in the way, his ego. "You're right. There was nothing I could have done to stop what happened. What I could've done was stay with you and to help you through it."

"Damn straight."

"I'm sorry. You have no idea how sorry I am. And how much I've missed you. Every day I've been here, all I've done is think about you. Even now, before I knew you were here, I was thinking about you on the way back from my hike. I would have spent every day for the rest of my life thinking of you, dreaming of you. Loving you."

Her breath caught, eyes going wide. "Loving me?"

"Olivia, I love you with every ounce of me. And I always will." He pulled her close before he could talk himself out of it, then kissed her as hard as he could. How had he ever imagined living without this? The thrill of tasting her lips, the way her body molded against his as she melted into the kiss. She threw her arms around his back and pulled him closer, holding on tight. The grip of a woman afraid of losing what she was holding. That wouldn't happen. He was never leaving her again.

"I love you." There were tears on her cheeks, but she was smiling when she opened her eyes to meet his. "I love you, too. That was what hurt the most. That I didn't get the chance to tell you." He responded by kissing her again, again, soaking in the sweetness, the softness. Drinking her in. Reveling in whatever it was that made her irresistible. And perfect for him.

His wolf roused, eager for more. For them to finally complete the bond. It wasn't easy, fighting against his natural instinct for her sake. He wanted this to be right for both of them.

As usual, she seemed to read his mind. "Like I said." She pulled back, still in his arms, and now there was a wicked twinkle in her eyes. "I'm off for the next couple of months. I have nowhere else to be but right here."

"Good thing, because you're not going anywhere." He scooped her up in his arms and she burst into giggles while he gave her a wolfish grin. "I have plans for you." She was still giggling when he carried her up the steps and into the cabin, barely taking time to kick the door closed behind him before rushing her up the stairs. They had waited long enough. He had longed for her until his body ached as much as his heart. There was no sense in wasting time now.

Yet instead of throwing her onto the bed, he laid her down gently. This was a gift, one he thought he'd lost forever. He kicked off his shoes, never breaking eye contact. "You're sure about this?"

She didn't answer in words, but instead unbuttoned her jeans and eased them over her legs, finally kicking them off onto the floor. His mouth went dry, his eyes taking in everything he'd missed these long, miserable weeks that had felt like years. He peeled off his shirt before lowering himself over her, almost pinning her to the bed.

She hooked a leg around his, drawing him closer, caressing his shoulders and back with one hand while the other curled around the back of his neck. "I do love you. I could live without anything but you."

He kissed her forehead, the tip of her nose, before finally finding her lips again. Her body moved under his like she was dancing to a song they would compose together. He matched her movements, welcoming the brush of her body against his already rigid dick. He lifted her t-shirt and she helped him work it over her head so he could leave a trail of kisses along her collarbones, then over the swells of her full breasts. Her sweet sighs pushed him on, encouraging him as much as her fingers running through his hair.

"Xavier... yes..." She whimpered when he found

one rosy nipple, drawing it between his teeth before lapping at it with his tongue. Like everything else about her, it was perfect.

He had imagined the way she'd react to this more times than he cared to remember, but he couldn't have imagined her sensuality. The way she writhed, her hips grinding in circles while her head rolled from side to side. An upward glance told him her eyes were closed, lips parted so endless sighs and soft moans could escape.

Dark desire unfurled in his core. His wolf, panting and growling, hungry for more. To see what else she could do. To hear her sighs turn to screams.

The brush of his hand over her stomach—and her sudden stiffening—brought him back to the present moment. He'd touched what was now a pink scar in the center of her abdomen. "Does it hurt?"

She shook her head, brows drawn together. "It's ugly, though."

"Who told you that? I don't think it's ugly." He lowered his head and placed a gentle kiss against it. "It's a symbol of your strength. You've been through so much and you're still standing. I'm proud of you."

She offered a tearful smile when he lifted his head. "Make love to me. Please." She held out her arms and he gladly sank into them, kissing her again, his hands roaming the length of her body until they were both practically in a frenzy. The scent of her arousal was enough to drive him crazy, while the way she ground herself against his erection almost hurt, it was so good.

He reached down between them, cupping her through her panties. She only groaned and tried to lower them to get them out of the way. He helped her, then returned his attention to her warm, wet folds, sinking his fingers into her.

She lifted her hips from the bed, riding his fingers, crying out when he found the bundle of nerves he knew would ache most of all. He stroked it, watching her every move. Every expression that floated across her face—concentration, determination, pleasure. There was a lot of that, and more to come.

"Xavier...!" She strained, hips rising higher before bucking hard. "I'm going to—!" One final cry and she collapsed against the mattress, shaking and whimpering his name. He closed his eyes, savoring the smell of her in the air. His mate. Only his.

His wolf's reaction was sudden and strong, that part of his consciousness almost exploding in a frenzy of need. He wouldn't be put off any longer, not after waiting all these weeks when he knew all along Olivia was meant to be theirs.

His hands shook and made him fumble with his belt. She helped him even though her hands shook, too. Their eyes met and he saw in them what he felt surging through him. Somehow he managed to take his jeans off without shredding them. Same with his boxer briefs, which Olivia slid over his hips and thighs before running her hands over his bare skin. When her nails dug into his flesh he growled, making her shiver.

He took himself in one hand and dragged his swollen head through her wetness. Now that they'd come this far, there was no hope of slowing down, not even for her sake. This went deeper than that. This was primal. Life itself. It wouldn't be denied any longer.

Which was why he plunged forward, entering her in one smooth stroke. Her eyes opened wide, a gasp tearing itself from her throat. "Did I hurt you?" He forced himself to stay still.

She shook her head. "Don't you dare stop."

He chuckled before pulling back and driving himself forward again. Again. Filling her, stretching her to accommodate his thickness. She locked her legs around his back, pulling him deeper and leaving him gritting his teeth in a desperate bid to hold on for her sake. Much more of that and this would come to an end too soon.

It didn't. They settled into a quick, steady rhythm like they'd been doing this for years. Was that how it was supposed to be? No fumbling, no awkwardness. Two souls meant for each other, made for each other.

He kissed her before moaning into her mouth. The familiar tingling began at the base of his spine, the sense of rushing to the finish. His wolf wanted nothing more, threatening to burst to the surface to claim what was his. *Mate. Mate.* The word repeated in his head almost loud enough to drown out the sounds of Olivia's approaching climax.

Her nails raked his back, her breath hot against his neck. "Xavier... oh, God... yes..." She tightened around him, almost like a vice gripping his shaft.

He lost control, thrusting mercilessly, his frenzied wolf taking over in those final moments until there was nothing left to do but sink his teeth into the flesh between her neck and shoulder. She arched against him with a sharp gasp before her muscles began to ripple, almost coaxing him into coming with her.

And he did, roaring out his release. A rush of

complete peace washed over him. The sense that finally, everything was the way it should be. He had everything he needed.

Finally, they both fell silent. There was nothing but the sound of their panting and the squeaking of bedsprings when he rolled away from her. She curled up next to him, her head on his chest. "I can't believe it."

"Can't believe what?" He expected her to come up with something about how profound that was. How it went beyond physical pleasure. How she couldn't have imagined it being as good as it was.

"I can't believe we waited so long to do that."

Of course. He laughed, pulling her into his arms and squeezing. "To tell the truth, neither can I."

"Good thing we have this whole cabin to ourselves, and all the time in the world to do whatever we want." She lifted her head, grinning up at him. "Because we have a lot of lost time to make up for."

"No amount of time will ever be enough." He kissed her, then chuckled as he brushed the hair away from her face. He would never get tired of looking at her face. "But we can sure try."

AFTERWORD

Click for more Ava Benton works!

Sign up for the newsletter to be notified of new releases.

Click on link for
Newsletter
or put this in your browser window:
mailerlite.com/webforms/landing/m7a8c5